HEATHER BOYD

USA TODAY BESTSELLING AUTHOR

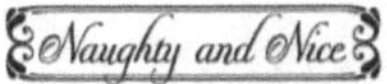

Love Me True

DEDICATION

For Tammy, Amy, Melissa & Michelle.
Thank you for always being there for me.

CHAPTER ONE

September, 1814
Devizes, Wiltshire

"I NOW PRONOUNCE you husband and wife." Those words concluded the wedding ceremony to cement the union of Lord Ramsbury and Mrs. Winifred Moore, widow, in holy matrimony but somewhere behind Lord Justin Greene, the bridegrooms' brother, a woman sobbed mournfully.

He did his best not to roll his eyes at the pitiful sound. To Justin's way of thinking, the happy groom did *not* deserve tears as he kissed his new wife soundly to wild applause. His brother, a rake many hoped to emulate, had recently taken to the idea of monogamy with astonishing single-mindedness. In fact, Justin had been quite shocked by the speed with which Tristan had accomplished his goal of marrying the local bookseller's daughter.

Of course, the former Mrs. Moore had better connections than most village girls. She was the niece of two current dukes, although not precisely on intimate terms, or even speaking terms, with them, and eminently qualified to her eventual elevation in rank to that of duchess.

And she did love his brother madly.

As the groom and blushing bride tripped past him, Justin followed along with the guests headed for the conveyances. He caught a glimpse of his mother and father, the often overbearing Duke and Duchess of Devizes, and returned their smiles. They'd gotten what they wanted—their eldest son and heir leg-shackled and five months away from delivering the first offspring.

The gaggle of delighted wedding guests followed the bride and groom along to the breakfast at Staplehurst Hall, giggling and laughing as if the world had just become sunnier. But for Justin, it was still filled with disappointments. Filled with things he couldn't have. He should shake off his black mood before his brother noticed. He was happy for the new couple. They were so very much in love.

However, shaking off his bad mood was next to impossible while the sniffing grew in volume behind his back.

He needed a drink.

As Justin entered Staplehurst Hall, the family seat of four generations of duke's and duchess', he took a detour to the library, heading for his father's hidden brandy to fortify himself in solitude against the long afternoon ahead.

A lone figure in drab muslin stood near the duke's desk polishing the smooth surface. "Oh, I'm sorry, Lord Justin. I'll be done in a moment." The saucy housemaid winked at him as she hurried to finish her chores. Justin watched the sway of her skirts, feeling an altogether wicked thought stir along with other parts.

"No rush, Lucy." Justin pulled the bottle he was after from its hiding place, and then leaned against the sideboard. He might need more than brandy to get through this day. "Tell me, do you have plans for later this evening?"

Lucy's eyes lit up with mischief. She paused in her chore to draw her shoulders back and remind him of the bounty lying beneath her plain, ugly gown. Clearly, the idea of helping him through the night appealed to her. Her tongue swiped over her bottom lip and bit it, sending a pleasant hum of lust through his body. As she released the plump pink flesh, Justin pushed off from the sideboard and stalked across the room, ready to steal a kiss before he had to face the afternoon festivities. But before he could sample the maid's charms, the door behind his back flew open.

Lucy bobbed a hasty curtsy.

"Is that my good brandy, Justin?"

So much for a pleasant interlude. Justin tipped his head towards the door to hasten Lucy's departure. "Yes, Father. Care for a snifter?"

Lucy gathered her dusting cloth and beat a quick retreat through the side door. Justin shrugged aside the lost opportunity to forget his disappointments. He would catch Lucy later and not finish with her until dawn smudged the horizon with the first sign of day.

"Don't mind if I do. Don't mind if I do." Leather creaked as his father sat. "What a day. At least now my Duchess can stop her carping on about heirs and such. But I must warn you— she's still dissatisfied with the living arrangements."

Justin suppressed a grin as he poured his father a drink. There was a very good reason Tristan and his new bride refused to move into Staplehurst Hall. They wanted privacy, and space to make love. His mother would definitely put a kink in their antics if she stumbled upon them in a state of undress.

Stumbling upon them *once* before the wedding had been bad enough for Justin. After that awkward sight, he'd taken to knocking his fist along the walls before he dreamed of stepping, or even looking, through an open doorway at the dower house. Those kinds of images he could do without.

He downed a quick mouthful then topped up his glass before turning to pass his father his drink. The duke was sprawled in regal splendor, a pleased smile on his features. He looked a great deal like himself—or Justin should say, *he* looked a great deal like his father. Except for that pleased smile. The duke had been this way since the marriage was announced a little under a month ago. The duchess was worse.

His father took a long swallow of brandy, rolling the flavor around his mouth as Justin prowled the library. When Justin finished his glass, he eyed the half-empty decanter. The wedding breakfast was sure to be a long and arduous celebration. Eighteen courses the last time Justin had listened to his mother's plans. One more snifter should do the trick and help him through the long, drawn out affair.

"You're next to marry you know," his father said suddenly.

Justin filled his glass to the brim and downed the contents in three swallows. Wonderful. With Tristan married, and well on the way to filling his nursery, Justin hadn't considered that his parents would focus on him so soon. He wasn't looking forward to marrying some sour-faced, well-dowered, connection-hungry young miss. All he desired was his poetry. "Is that so?" He tried very hard to sound bored with the idea, hoping his father would find another subject soon.

"Well, yes. A quick marriage is just the thing. I won't be putting up with Tristan's nonsense again. No chance of cold feet that way."

Thanks to the two glasses of brandy—well, maybe two and a half—Justin didn't panic quite as he would if completely sober. He did experience some discomfort, though, that he wouldn't get to marry the girl of his dreams. Not when she loved another. He would forever be the man she couldn't see. Justin reached for the decanter again.

Another drink sent the room tripping and when his father clapped him a stunning blow to his shoulder, Justin stumbled forward.

"Let's get this over with," his father said.

"Otherwise, my duchess will come looking for us."

Heaven help them, then. He forced a smile to his lips. "Of course."

Justin turned unsteadily for the library door and followed in his father's wake, entering the noisy hall. One hundred guests filled the room, most already seated and consuming his father's fine wines. Justin threaded through the crowd until he found his assigned table. To his surprise, and considerable horror, he found himself seated beside Miss Claribel Wheaton, the haughtiest young lady he knew, and across from the stuffy Earl of Edenbray, his new sister's estranged cousin.

And Miss Wheaton was still sniffling her grief over his brother's marriage.

The brunette, small and well-rounded, shared more opinions than anyone he knew. Normally, she appeared the perfectly flawless debutant. But not today. Today the little woman couldn't keep her countenance. A broken heart could render even the strongest disposition useless.

As he sat, Justin signaled for the footman to fill his glass and then he turned to his companion, resigned to another awkward conversation. "Miss Wheaton, you look lovely."

The watering debutante's nose wrinkled

with distaste, and then she buried it in her handkerchief again. Justin shrugged, determined to ignore the snub. Really, what could one say to comfort a broken heart? In his experience, it was better to pretend the whole farce of falling in love had never happened in the first place.

Justin crooked his finger at the footman. "Bring a bottle from the lower shelf, and keep them coming."

The footman obliged and when the other guests were amply distracted, he topped up Miss Wheaton's glass with something containing a little more kick than that served to most in attendance.

The woman lifted her nose from her scrap of lace and eyed her now brimming glass. Her gaze skittered sideways. "Thank you."

"Always happy to assist." Justin admired the rich liquid. "However, this might be a tad too strong for you. Don't feel you need to drink it all."

As if challenged by his words, Miss Wheaton sat up straighter and took a swallow. Unfortunately, she gulped the liquid instead of sipping and sputtered into her handkerchief, no doubt because the liquid burned her throat.

"'Tis much better to savor than to rush, sweetheart."

Justin scowled at his own words. The reminder of his brother's most recent taunt, that he had little skill at charming women, angered him. What he didn't bother to explain to his smug brother was that one woman was much like the next, especially since pleasing the woman that mattered most to him remained far beyond his reach. He would please *her* if she gave him half a chance. However, the woman he loved barely acknowledged his existence. To find relief, he dabbled with ladies who'd rather tumble into bed than talk. But their charms were pale substitutes for the woman he'd never have.

Justin kept drinking and topping up his companion's glass with each unending course served until Miss Wheaton disappeared from his side without a word. *Haughty minx.* He hoped she nursed a terrible head for the disrespect of not speaking more than two words to him.

He glanced around. Since the hour was late, the revelers were a merry bunch, forming little groups to suit themselves. His brother and his new bride were gone. Justin lurched to his feet. He'd not be missed by those present—most were too wrapped up in their own conversations to notice—so he took himself off to find more pleasurable entertainment. Lucy might just be waiting him in his chambers if he were lucky, or would be joining him there very soon.

All he had to do was remember where the hell his chambers were.

After a few false starts, Justin fell through his bedchamber door. Would he ever find this new bedchamber easily? Probably not. The move to Tristan's old chambers had been his mother's idea. She'd wanted to freshen up the family wing in the hope of enticing Tristan and Winifred to move into the Hall. Dumping him in the now empty east wing, and away from his mother's unpredictable visits, suited him just fine.

Justin stripped his coat, waistcoat and shirt from his chest in the dark, relieved to be free of the restrictions. He sat—stumbled, to put it more accurately—and after a few blunders, managed to remove his boots. His hands fell to his formal breeches and he tugged the buttons undone. A woman's heavy sigh and the rustle of sheets reached his ears.

Despite his over indulgence tonight, his prick thickened at the sound.

Lucy awaited him already. She must have shirked more of her duties tonight to share his bed at this hour. If it wasn't his bed she'd been gracing on occasion since his twentieth year, she'd probably have been dismissed for her outright laziness.

Justin kicked off his remaining clothes and crawled under the covers.

Lucy cuddled into him and sought his lips in an ardent closed-mouthed kiss. Her attempt to appear virginal tonight amused him, but the press of her hardened nipples spoke loudly of her desires. He liked her games. He liked the pretense that she hadn't spread her legs for anyone but him. But as her wine-scented breath puffed over his lips, he scowled. She'd obviously helped herself to the refreshments laid out for the guests tonight and, by the scent tickling his nose, she had also sampled a guest's perfume, too.

He'd censure her about it in the morning, but for now she seemed altogether too delicious to ignore. He set his lips to her neck to lightly nip at her skin. Lucy shuddered and moaned with almost believable surprise, building the fiction that she'd never lain in a man's arms. She'd missed her true calling in life, it seemed. She could have performed on the stage.

Justin pulled Lucy atop him. She stiffened and squirmed, rubbing her breasts against his chest awkwardly as if unused to the position. When he hastened to kiss her into compliance, she wriggled around until she was comfortably draped over his body, putting his stiff prick against her thigh. Justin tugged a little more until he lay primed and ready to slide into place. His delicious bundle whimpered.

"Shh, love. You know your safe with me." He pushed her long, heavy hair back from her face and cupped her cheek. He couldn't see her face clearly and he brushed his lips across her cheek. "I'll give you everything you need. I promise."

Lucy twisted suddenly and planted her lips tightly against his. Surprised by the sudden move, Justin kissed her back, pressing his tongue into the seam of her lips until they parted. The taste of her was heaven. Blind desire washed over him, leaving him breathless. He wrapped his arms around her and plundered her mouth, desperate to join with her in every way possible. He slid his palm down her back, over the firm round swell of her bottom and grasped one thigh. He inched her legs apart until she opened to him.

Justin flexed his hips, aligning himself to thrust inside. With Lucy's hands threaded through his hair, her mouth open over his, he pushed in gently—as if they'd never done this before. As if she was in truth virginal—not wanton and hungry for pleasure. Lucy tensed, clamping her lower muscles tightly around him.

Another thrust seated him inside her and his world shrank to just the pair of them.

God she was a good actress. Her initial whimper had sounded authentic. The tight control she used on her sex to simulate a novice in the bedchamber could almost fool a man, but as he slid in and out her rough pant gave her away.

This was no virginal, scared miss. This was a woman swept away by desire. Justin rolled them until he hovered above. He braced himself on his elbows, holding his weight suspended and gave himself over to the delicious illusion they'd woven.

CHAPTER TWO

THE BED ROCKED ENOUGH to make Clarry sick. She clutched the sheet tightly against her face and tried to block out the insistent voice nagging her to get up.

"Come on, luv. Mrs. Gillard will have your head if she catches you sleeping the day away," the deep male voice insisted beside her ear.

Clarry's head exploded with a pain so great she moaned aloud. A hard smack landed on her bottom—her very bare bottom.

"On your feet sleepy."

Clarry opened one eye and lowered the sheet a fraction. The unfamiliar room about her brought a gasp from her lips. She wasn't at home or anywhere she recognized. The bed dipped behind her and then she heard movement, a man's cough and the sound of pouring water. What was he doing? And what was she doing here?

She rubbed her temple as her memory of last night returned. She'd wanted to speak with Lord Ramsbury before it was too late. Obviously she'd found him but that didn't explain why she was in his bed. Why was Lord Ramsbury going about his day as if having her in his bed was an ordinary event?

She shut her eyes and ran her hand over her skin beneath the sheet. Her bare skin. She glanced down at herself. Naked. As in the day she was born, naked. Clarry wriggled until she was cocooned in the crisp white sheets, feeling colder than she had her entire life. What had she done? And what had she had done to her?

A touch skimmed up her leg—warm, hard, and somehow comforting. "Time to rise." The covers were wrenched from her grip. "Sleeping beau . . ."

Clarry squeaked and snapped her eyes closed, but not before she glimpsed a broad and shockingly bare male chest. So, she'd done it. She'd captured Lord Ramsbury's attention on his wedding night. She should be pleased to have stolen the groom from his new bride on such an important night. But her victory rang flat. To put it quite plainly—she couldn't remember even speaking to the viscount, let alone climbing into his bed.

"Sweet Jesus." The sheet caressed her as her companion inched it down her body, revealing more of her to the light than she imagined necessary. She reached for it and grappled with two strong hands, winning but only after pinching his skin.

"Well, this is an astonishing surprise. Good morning, Clarry."

Clarry risked opening one eye again and spied Lord Justin leaning over her, a foolish grin spread across his face. She scrambled away, dragging the sheet with her for protection. "Get away from me."

His brilliant smile dimmed. "What game are you playing?"

"What game are you? What gives you the right to be here?"

The smile disappeared altogether. "Every right. This is my bedchamber. And that is my bed you're hiding in."

"You don't belong here. Your chamber is on the other side of the house." Clarry glanced around nervously. "Isn't it?"

"I moved." The clipped words came out from between his clenched teeth and Clarry hugged herself tighter. She glanced around frantically and spied her clothes from last night laid across the far chair. But to reach them, she had to pass Lord Justin—the naked rake that appeared to have taken her virtue in his brother's place.

Clarry pressed her hands to her face to hide her distress. Good grief, she had thrown herself at the wrong man. She rubbed her temples with her fingertips, listening to Lord Justin move away. Why couldn't she remember Lord Justin's seduction? Usually she had an excellent memory. She had never, ever, encouraged *that* man to call on her. Or smiled or laughed at his many jokes. Really, had last nights revelry clouded her mind that badly?

Or perhaps her disguised state had turned off her sense of self-preservation. A rake like Lord Justin would certainly take what was offered and more without regard to her inebriated state. Well, she was done for now—a fallen woman with no hope for the brilliant future of which she'd dreamed. Even as deeply inebriated as she must have been, how could she not have recognized and refused Lord Justin's advances last night? He was nowhere near as charming as his brother—the man she loved. The one she'd risked scandal for to prove they were meant to be together.

Lord Justin returned and pressed a wet

something to the back of her fingers. "This will help settle your head."

Clarry took the cloth and the cool moisture did seem to help. When it was too warm to be useful she let her hand fall. She was doomed. Lord Justin took it away and, when he'd moved further across the room, Clarry risked a second peek. His broad, smooth back, more muscular than she'd imagined, gave way to a sleek pair of buttocks and long limbs. Clarry closed her mouth as Lord Justin turned and she couldn't stop a squeak from escaping her lips again. He wasn't wearing anything at all. Yet he walked toward her without any sign of discomfort.

He held out the cloth and Clarry quickly snatched it from his hand to press the blessed coolness against her heated skin.

The mattress dipped as he sat close beside her. "I take it from your reaction that you were not expecting to have shared last night with me. You thought that this was to be my brother's room last night, didn't you?"

Clarry nodded swiftly and instantly regretted that decision. Her skull would explode at any moment. She licked her lips nervously. Could a mistake of this magnitude be hushed up with no consequences? She sincerely hoped so.

Lord Justin didn't move and he didn't speak

for a long time. When Clarry lifted her gaze, she found him slumped. One glance at his face, however, closed her eyes. She'd never witnessed a bleaker expression on a man. He looked as if someone had stolen his inheritance.

"There is nothing else for it now." He stood and then bent to lift his shirt from the floor, exposing his bare bottom to her shocked eyes. "Get dressed as best you can. I will finish lacing you up. After I've made arrangements, I will take you home."

The emotionless tone of Lord Justin's voice sent her from his bed and she hastily dropped the sheet to pull on her clothes. Although her skull pounded, she managed to drag her chemise over her head, and then wobbled on shaky legs as she picked up her corset. How she had loosened the tight strings without aid escaped her. Could she even get back into it without the help of a maid? She managed to fit the stiff garment around her and then reached for the laces at her back. Lord Justin stepped close behind and took them from her grip. In next to no time, her breasts were bound tightly again.

Of course he would know his way about a corset. The thought irritated her more than it should. Lord Justin was a rake, and was rumored to bed any woman who smiled his way.

A very good reason to have steered clear of him in the past. A shame she hadn't remembered to do so last night.

"All done."

Clarry took a breath and then another. At least he hadn't tightened the laces too far so as to strangle her as her companion frequently did. The thought of Bethany Gainsford's scowl chilled her. Her companion would ring a peal over her head for this lapse of judgment and regale her with yet another tale of some nameless woman's mistake in tempting a terrible man. Now, of course, Bethany could use Clarry as her example.

Her gown fluttered over her head, and Lord Justin settled the material in place without a word. As he did up the tiny pearl buttons with agonizing slowness, his breath washed over her bare shoulder and she hastened to tug the material higher. "I can't see my stockings."

"Leave them." Lord Justin's voice dipped deep, and she turned around. His staff peeked out from under his fine linen shirt in a most disconcerting way. At this proximity, she had time to notice a thousand intimate details about Lord Justin. Despite the situation, his thick member, veins standing out in stark relief, intrigued her. She didn't know the correct term but she couldn't drag her gaze away.

Lord Justin turned abruptly. He threw off the shirt he was wearing, leaving his bare back facing her and pulled on smalls, a new shirt and trousers, affording Clarry a completely unfamiliar glimpse into a gentleman's life. Lord Justin was quite particularly attentive in his dressing habits, as if he was nervous, fussing with three cravats until they were perfectly tied. His gaze met hers in the tall oval mirror as he secured his cravat with a jade pin. Her chest tightened.

Despite her earlier opinion and desire to avoid him in the past, he was a handsome man. But she disliked him for his rakish ways, favoring his brother's steady character instead. Lord Ramsbury's smile set Clarry's heart to wing whereas Lord Justin's planted her feet on disturbingly unsteady ground.

Clarry looked away first. She felt embarrassed for having shared a bed with a man she cared nothing for, or he for her when she thought about it. Yet he was being so kind about her blunder that she wondered what he was thinking and whether he'd tell his friends of his successful seduction. As he settled a waistcoat in place and started doing up the buttons, she took a step toward him.

He scowled. "You cannot face the duchess like that."

"Face the duchess?" Foolishly, Clarry shook her head and winced again. "I thought you were going to help me return home?"

"I am. But not until I can speak to my parents about our marriage. I want to ensure that they will support the match."

"Marriage?" Clarry parroted, sagging into the nearest chair as her legs gave way. She couldn't bear to marry a man she didn't love. And she did *not* love Lord Justin. She loved his brother with her whole heart. "Oh, no, I couldn't possibly marry *you*," she protested.

Lord Justin stalked across the room and dragged her to her feet. "Well, how did you think this would end? Did you think I would bed an innocent and then discard her as if she were no better than a common whore?"

When Clarry didn't answer, Justin gave her a little shake. She cleared her throat. "Of course, I did. We hardly know each other, but I've heard enough gossip about you. I know how you live your life. Debauchery and vice at every turn. I won't live like that."

Couldn't he see how miserable she'd be as his wife?

Justin's fingers tightened on her arm. "You don't understand the first thing about me, Miss Wheaton. It appears as if you are in for something of a shock."

Clarry glanced about the room, looking for a door to escape through. That didn't sound pleasant or painless.

Lord Justin set his hands to her shoulders and forcibly turned her in the chair. "Sit."

Was he planning to make her his prisoner now? But Lord Justin merely threaded his fingers through her hair, combing through snarls until she felt no pain. Then with deft twists of his fingers, her hair landed on her head and he reached for the pins she'd left in a pile last night.

When he was done, he dragged her upright to face him. He tugged tucked a few missed strands behind her ear and nudged her mouth shut.

"Time to face the Duchess."

CHAPTER THREE

JUSTIN DRAGGED Claribel out of his bedroom and marched them down the hall toward the ducal apartments. Although he knew this marriage was not what she wanted, he was honor bound to make it right and save her reputation. To save her from her own foolishness. He could not believe she would stoop so low as to try to seduce a man clearly in love with another woman. And married to her now, too. The thought made him nauseous.

Although he hadn't realized until this morning that it wasn't Lucy in his bed last night, Clarry had been heaven in his arms. She had responded with such delightful enthusiasm, and her passionate responses and demands had inflamed him.

But it was all a lie. Those responses had

been for his brother, Tristan. A man who had never once shown her any partiality that he could remember, despite Clarry's obvious attempts to capture his attention. Justin had watched from the sidelines, heart sinking with each encounter until he couldn't stand to watch anymore.

Loving someone who didn't love you back hurt.

And now they would suffer together in polite silence until death parted them. Not even he had dared write such a mournful ending for one of his character's lives.

Out of the corner of his eye, he caught sight of Clarry holding her temple. Justin instantly slowed his pace to match her shorter strides. He'd forgotten her head probably beat like a drum from her over indulgence of last night. Perhaps he was partially to blame for her state this morning, but he'd forgotten any thought of guilt or complicity the moment she admitted she'd been planning to spend the night in his newly married brother's bed. Of all the foolish things to do. But the deed was done, beyond her power to correct, and he hoped to God he could survive this unholy union.

Justin stopped before the corridor leading to his mother's private chambers and turned to

Claribel. She winced as she looked up at him and he moved her so she rested against the wall behind a potted plant so they might have more privacy should anyone stumble upon them. "When we see Her Grace I want you to let me do all the talking. No matter what I say, just nod your head and agree with me. Is that understood?"

Claribel's eyes filled with tears. "What are you going to tell her?"

He wasn't in the mood for tears. Not from this scheming chit, and certainly not after this morning's revelations. "Certainly not every-thing. Not even a quarter." He grasped her arm, tucking her against his side. "But it must be done immediately if we have a hope of being believed. Come on. Smile Miss Wheaton. Your reputation depends on it."

As the two footmen positioned outside the ducal apartments came into view, Claribel clutched his arm. "I don't think I can do this."

"Don't be ridiculous, Clarry. Marriage is the only choice you have."

Justin nodded to the servants. "I'd like to see my mother immediately. Would you ask if she is prepared for visitors?"

"Of course, Lord Justin." The tallest man tapped on the door and stepped into the an-techamber leading to his mother's bedchamber.

After a brief rush of words with his mother's maid, they were ushered inside. Claribel dropped his arm immediately and moved to the fireplace, rubbing her arms as she went. There would be a lengthy wait, of course. His mother was notoriously fussy about being seen in perfect looks. So when the door burst open and his mother rushed in, he was so surprised that his hastily put together announcement flew out of his mind. He gulped to clear his throat. "Mother. You're already up?"

"Well, of course I am, my darling boy. I'm standing here, am I not?"

She took another step into the room then her eyes widened as they landed on Claribel. "Mother, I have some wonderful news."

The duchess clutched her hands together at her waist. "You found her first. Thank heavens. Now that she's been located, unharmed, we can return her home. Her father is beside himself with worry."

Justin glanced at Claribel and noticed she bit her lip. Was she wondering if it were possible to get out of this mess without anyone knowing where she'd spent the night? Her mouth opened and a squeak of sound emerged. Justin shook his head to silence her. "Mother, you can be the first to congratulate me. Miss Wheaton has consented to become my wife."

The silence in the chamber was loud enough to deafen them all. Then the duchess clucked her tongue and turned away, sinking into a chair with a sigh. "I hardly think such a drastic action is necessary, Justin. No doubt Miss Wheaton fell asleep in some out of the way place. There is no need to offer marriage for a miscalculation on her part."

Since his mother disliked Miss Wheaton quite strongly she would, of course, try to save him from what she saw as a potential entrapment. If she knew the truth of last night, he hated to think what she'd do to them both. The duchess could make Clarry's life here at the Hall hell on earth if she learned what her real aim had been for the previous night.

Justin set his hands to his hips. "There is every need, Your Grace. We wish to marry."

His mother glanced at him sharply, eyes taking in his fresh appearance and then Claribel's rumpled state. Her eyes narrowed. "Is that so? And whose idea is that?"

Justin braced himself. "Mine."

The duchess glanced between them again, a frown softening slowly into a less hostile expression. She sighed heavily. "Your father will need to see you immediately, Justin. Leave Miss Wheaton here with me while the pair of you debate the consequences of your rash decision."

"Of course."

Although he loathed leaving Clarry alone with his mother, he did need to speak to his father, especially if there was a search underway. Justin kissed his mother's cheek and then turned to Clarry. Her face had drained of color and her hand rested on the back of a chair for support.

Justin crossed the room and set one hand to her shoulder. "I'll be back soon, my love."

He dropped a kiss to her cheek then drew back to see how she reacted. Her skin flushed a delicious pink. He hoped that blush was from pleasure and not embarrassment. With one more squeeze to her shoulder, Justin strode out the door and headed for his father's study. He entered without knocking and found not just his father, but Mr. Wheaton, Lord Edenbray and his brother Tristan arguing loudly about Clarry's disappearance. This was going to be awkward.

"Where the hell have you been!" his father bellowed.

"Visiting with Her Grace." Justin crossed the room. "May I have a private word with you, Father?"

"Later, boy, later. Miss Wheaton is missing and must be found." His father turned back to

Mr. Wheaton who was consulting a large map of the district.

Justin cleared his throat. "Ah, I should tell you about Miss Wheaton first. She's with Her Grace at present."

Both men turned to stare at him, their expressions hot enough to bore holes into his head. Somewhat tardily, Justin remembered that neither man had a reputation for keeping his countenance when faced with unpleasantness.

Clarry's father closed the gap between them. Tall, ginger haired and renowned for his quick temper, Mr. Wheaton added invisible daggers to his chest. "She's where?"

Justin swallowed before speaking. "She is with Her Grace. I just left her there."

"Jus—" his brother began—"what have you done?"

He'd not be explaining a damn thing to Tristan since he was the one who'd led him—albeit inadvertently—into this mess. "I'd like to request an interview with you too, Mr. Wheaton, at your earliest convenience."

Mr. Wheaton scowled, teeth grinding together, but he did nod his head. "Am I to assume there might be some unseemly haste to your need for this discussion?"

Justin dipped his head cautiously, wondering how the older man would take the news.

Mr. Wheaton scowled and then he sat himself down to wait.

"For Gods sake, Justin—" his father huffed —"I said choose a bride quickly, but this is ridiculous. Have you no sense of timing?"

"No, Father, apparently none at all."

His father scowled and then ushered Lord Edenbray from the chamber. Tristan settled against a wall, arms over his chest, but their father hooked his arm and hauled him toward the door. "Out. Go back to your wife."

"But—" Tristan began.

Their father slammed the door shut in Tristan's face and the crash gave Justin chills.

"Justin," his brother shouted through the wood, "I'll be back to speak with you later."

Oh, wonderful. Did Tristan expect him to relate all the details of his future wife's affections? Justin would not share that information with her one true love even on his death bed.

Well, this was it. This was the most important negotiation of his life. He had to fool them both into thinking he and Clarry were so madly in love that they might agree with his request to be married by special license to save her reputation. If only that could be remotely true.

Clarry's father sat forward. "Explain yourself young man."

He met Mr. Wheaton's gaze direct. "We are in love."

Mr. Wheaton scoffed. "The only thing my daughter is in love with is herself. Young man, you've made a foolish choice for a bride."

He snapped his mouth shut as his father started coughing into his fist. That wasn't the type of comment Justin had expected either. "I'm sure you're mistaken. Your daughter is everything a man could want for a wife."

Except for the small problem of her being in love with his happily married brother.

Mr. Wheaton looked on him with pity. "My wife spoiled my daughter to an alarming degree. Despite my attempts to nurture more serious interests, she has the attention span of a flea. She will bore you to tears within a week."

Justin glanced at his father to find him wide eyed. What the hell kind of interview was this? He had expected Mr. Wheaton to rail at him for ruining his daughter, not to be the object of pity. He found Mr. Wheaton's lack of concern astonishing. "Nevertheless, I wish to marry her as soon as possible. We'd also like to marry by special license rather than waiting for the banns to be called."

While his father raised an eyebrow at Justin's obvious haste, Mr. Wheaton nodded in agreement. "Probably a good idea. The flighty chit may very well try to abscond during the night as it is. I'd make a point to lock the doors at night. However, if she does make a run for it, I'm not chasing after her. I've had enough of her antics to last me a life time." Mr. Wheaton pointed a finger at him. "She's your problem now."

Good God. This was a side of Clarry's father that he'd never imagined existed. Oh, he knew Mr. Wheaton was a gruff man like his father, but at least the duke proved he had a heart now and again. Mr. Wheaton's callous disregard for his daughter's battered reputation angered him. "Well, if that is the case then perhaps you would allow her to stay at Staplehurst Hall until the wedding. I'm sure my mother would be glad for the company."

Justin glanced at his father and prayed he wouldn't contradict his invitation. His father nodded sagely. "Yes. Yes. My duchess enjoys the company of the younger set. Claribel will have ample chaperonage, too, since Lady Armitage is still in residence."

Mr. Wheaton snorted loudly then glanced in Justin's direction. "Hardly matters now, does it? Do whatever the hell you wish with her. I'll return to sign the contract and for the wedding."

The duke held up his hands. "I assure you, your daughter will be sleeping on the other side of the house, far from my son until the wedding."

Mr. Wheaton shook his head in disgust and speared Justin with a harsh glance. "Don't say I didn't warn you if she makes you miserable."

With that, Mr. Wheaton stalked out, shutting the door loudly behind him.

Justin stared after him in shock. Damnation! He turned to his father.

The duke had sunk into his chair and was studying him intently. "Explain."

Justin hated lying to his father. He'd never been very good at it in the past but he had to make the attempt. "Miss Wheaton and I have discovered that we suit quite well. Be happy for me."

His father shook his finger as he sat forward. "Yesterday you almost bolted from my presence when we discussed finding you a wife. I highly doubt that a few short hours have changed your opinion of the wedded state."

Oh, if only his father knew how those hours had changed him. "Sometimes a moment of clarity is all it takes."

His father pursed his lips. "We should discuss living arrangements before your mother sets her heart on what you don't want." He twisted to pull a ledger from a shelf nearby and flipped the pages open. "The house in Sussex is presently vacant and in good repair, or the property in Cheshire could do very well for you, too."

Justin's heart sank. "You're banishing me for marrying Miss Wheaton?"

His father closed the ledger. "No. No, of course not. I simply expected you to want the same privacy as your brother. As you know, your mother is prone to meddling. If I didn't need Tristan close by, and he could convince Winifred to leave her father behind, he'd have taken the Cheshire property."

"Father, I have no desire at all to move away from Staplehurst Hall. All of Clarry's friends are here. I would not like to deprive her of place in society. She will come to hate me more if I take her away."

His father stood and circled the desk. When he placed a hand over Justin's shoulder and squeezed, Justin almost jumped away. "And why would Miss Wheaton—a woman who you claim has happily accepted your proposal of marriage—hate you more, Justin. Exactly what happened last night?"

Justin looked down. Of all the times for his father to show his concern, this was the worst possible moment. He didn't want to think about why Clarry had to marry him. For the moment, he wanted to live in the dream. But his father appeared determined to get an answer if his expression was any indication. Justin had never managed to hold out for long. He squared his shoulders. "Neither of us got what we expected. But it's done and I know my duty."

CHAPTER FOUR

CLARRY'S HAND shook as she raised the gold rimmed teacup to her lips and took a hesitant sip. Quite frankly, if not for the duchess's stern gaze commanding her to drink, Clarry didn't think she could. Her belly rebelled over the intake of nourishment. She was so humiliated that she had to marry Lord Justin.

She was to marry a rake for heaven's sake.

A man who cared for nothing but his own pleasure. She would become a laughing stock.

Clarry carefully lowered her teacup, pleased that her hand didn't shake too badly. With the duchess watching her every move—and making no attempt at polite conversation—she had never been more uncomfortable. Not even finding that she'd shared a bed with Lord Justin compared to the duchess's hostile scrutiny.

The door behind her opened. "I say, Dezzie, are you out of your mind?"

Clarry knew that voice, and her heart sank. Lady Armitage, the duchess's elder sister, didn't care for her either. This would be more than a little awkward.

The duchess waved her hand in Clarry's direction. "I wish I were. This is a tragedy."

Clarry turned to acknowledge Lady Armitage and wanted to sink through the floor. It was well known that Lady Armitage was inordinately fond of her nephews, and she appeared outraged. "What can be done?"

"Nothing. He has thrown his heart on the altar of shattered dreams and even now faces the overwhelming consequences."

Lady Armitage sank into a chair close to her sister and took hold of her hand. "Moving. Very moving, Dezzie dear. How long did it take you to compose?"

The duchess squinted at the clock on the mantle. "Ooh, twenty minutes or so. A good lament needs only the right motivation. Justin should like it very much."

Lady Armitage patted her sister's hand again. "Justin has a fine mind and romantic soul. I cannot wait to see how this drama influences his future work."

The duchess sighed. "Let us hope this disturbance will not affect his art too greatly. His latest project is at a critical stage."

When both ladies focused their attention on Clarry, she squirmed. "Does Lord Justin dabble in poetry and writing?"

Both Lady Armitage and the duchess shook their heads at her. When they didn't comment, she flushed in embarrassment. She should not have admitted her ignorance of something so obviously important to Lord Justin. If they were to marry under normal circumstances, she might have been aware of his penchant for the written word.

Yet she'd never spared him a second glance. The first had always been to check if his brother joined him in town.

When the two sisters spoke of yesterday's wedding without including her, Clarry didn't mind. She glanced down at her hands and let their words lull her. But the torture of waiting for Justin's return would drive her mad. She raised her head and cast a surreptitious glance at the mantle clock. She'd been with the duchess an hour. What could possibly be keeping him so long?

As if summoned by her thoughts, the door handle turned and Justin strode in. His gaze traveled the room and settled, not on Clarry, but on his aunt. "There you are, Auntie dearest. Have you heard my good news?"

Lady Armitage stood and framed his face with her wrinkled and bejeweled hands. "I have."

He pressed a quick kiss to her forehead in return, and whispered something Clarry couldn't catch. The countess's fingers slid from his face and she shrugged. "If you wish it."

"Of course I do." His gaze finally landed on Clarry and her skin flamed. "Clarry, your father wants to see you. Come along."

She scrambled to her feet, dropped curtseys to the duchess and Lady Armitage then rushed to join Lord Justin. Despite the horror of the morning, she breathed easier being nearer to him. Once within reach, Lord Justin captured her fingers and led her outside. They walked for what seemed an eternity then he led her into another chamber. But the elegant chamber appeared empty of her father. They were all alone.

When Clarry turned to face him, she was startled to find him standing so close. She looked up and up, but Lord Justin lowered his head and captured her lips. Shock held her immobile at first. Lord Justin appeared to be well versed in the art of kissing and her legs trembled as he persisted. His hand stole around her back, burning her skin through the gown as he pulled her closer against his chest.

Clarry raised her hands to hold him at bay, but the delicious assault of his mouth curled her fingertips into his clothing. His tongue licked along the seam of her mouth and she opened her lips with a sigh.

Lord Justin kissed with considerable talent. No wonder she'd succumbed so easily last night. He invaded the recesses of her mouth, tasting and sharing more of himself than she thought possible. His hands stole lower, curling around her bottom and forcing a squeak from her lips. Lord Justin released her, his expression one she couldn't fathom.

When he sighed and scrubbed his hand over his mouth, Clarry quickly lowered her eyes. That he regretted kissing her was clear. That she'd enjoyed the experience and wanted more kisses didn't bode well for her peace of mind. She loved Lord Ramsbury. How could she want Lord Justin's kisses?

Confused Clarry took two paces back. "I thought you were taking me to see my father."

Lord Justin scrubbed his hand through his hair, a gesture she'd rarely seen him do. "He's left the Hall already."

Clarry dropped her gaze to the floor. She'd

thought it surprising that her father would wait for her after the events of last night. She'd hoped he wouldn't be too angry. According to him, she'd grown too much like her mother for his comfort. He'd expect her to make her own way home or not to bother at all. Just like her mother hadn't all those years ago. It no longer surprised her that Mother had chosen to find sanctuary outside her marriage. Her father was a difficult man to please and unforgiving of failure.

Her lover of last night moved closer. "Clarry, your father has agreed to you moving into the Hall prior to our wedding as my mother's guest. From today, you live here."

She shook her head. "What about Miss Gainsford?"

Lord Justin settled onto the edge of the table and folded his arms across his chest. He looked so much bigger than a moment ago. "Who is Miss Gainsford?"

Clarry did her best not to be intimidated. "Bethany Gainsford is my companion. Father will surely end her employment as he has no need of her services now."

Lord Justin cocked his head to the side and studied her without speaking, exactly as the duchess had done earlier. Honestly, could these people not say exactly what was on their minds?

Must they intimidate with every gesture and look. But she was concerned about what would become of Bethany. The woman had no one else, no family or friends, that Clarry could determine. And she had an unhealthy attitude to her freedom. It had taken all of Clarry's persistence to keep her as her companion. The woman had no one else.

As Lord Justin studied her, she took a risk and stepped toward him. "Bethany has very little in funds. I'd hate to see her cast out the way I fear my father will. I'd like to help her."

Lord Justin's weary sigh made her heart flutter.

He nodded slowly. "Very well. I'll go see your father directly and make the necessary arrangements for Miss Gainsford to enter employment here. Is there anything else you must have?"

The tone of his words hinted he thought her too demanding already. Pain tightened her chest. "No. No, there is nothing else. I'm concerned only for Bethany."

"Of course." Lord Justin stood, towering above her without a word.

Clarry hastily looked down, but was confronted by the broad expanse of his chest and the fine silk waistcoat that she'd clung to just moments before. Given the way he'd kissed her, she wondered whether she'd be spending her nights alone prior to the wedding. What surprised her more was wondering whether she wanted to. He did kiss rather well, and now that her head no longer pained her, she could remember parts of last night. It hadn't been *all* bad, or even mostly bad.

She glanced up as Lord Justin lowered his head and kissed her again. This time she was a little more prepared for his kisses. They left her gasping, writhing almost. His large hands curled around her waist and hoisted her up into his arms. With her feet dangling inches from the floor she had to hold onto him.

Clarry wrapped her fingers around his shoulders as he deepened the kiss, threatening to consume her with his desire. She did her best to keep her head, but her body thrummed with sensations she couldn't name. Suddenly, Clarry found herself sitting atop Lord Justin on the pale pink lounge. She gazed at him in surprise as he fumbled with her skirts until he touched her bare skin.

She remembered his hands from last night. The warm swipe of his fingers over her leg reminded her that his touch had been delicious, too, so she settled more comfortably astride him.

Lord Justin cradled her skull one-handed as he fumbled beneath her gown. After a moment, he grasped her hips and shifted her position. It took a moment to realize that Lord Justin intended to make love to her. Now. His slow slide into her body took her breath away and she gazed at him in wonder. How heavenly he felt. His hand curled over her shoulder and pushed down until she felt sure he couldn't fill her any further.

She blinked and glanced down, but with her skirts in the way she really couldn't see a thing. Their eyes met as he lifted her, and then lowered her down his length. Clarry clutched at his shoulders as the strangest sensations rippled through her. She'd never imagined making love would feel like this. She ached between her legs to be sure. But it wasn't a pain she wanted to make go away. She wanted more. But had no idea how to get it.

Lord Justin had closed his eyes as he loved her and she watched his face, noticing tension holding his mouth immobile. Clarry leaned forward to kiss that tense mouth and his eyes flew wide open. Instead of kissing her back, he flipped them so she landed on her back with him hovering over. With the change of position, Clarry was assaulted with a hundred other compelling sensations. His heat, his scent—the pressure of him against her hips. She widened her legs and clung to the man who intended to marry her.

That seemed to be agreeable because he sped up his thrusts, increasing her pleasure tenfold. As his body pressed hard against her, Clarry tensed, and then her world stopped. She burned, she writhed, she whimpered as the most incredible sensations swamped her.

When she opened her eyes, Lord Justin was watching her, a satisfied grin on his face.

His length was still buried within her, and he thrust hard into her again and again then buried his face in her neck and moaned. Clarry settled her hands on Justin's back and held him close. Perhaps marriage to a rake wouldn't be all that bad if he could make love to her like that every now and then. No, marriage to him could be nice so long as she remembered him incapable of tender emotions.

Justin levered up on one arm and stared at her. But this time his stare was more comfortable. They had shared something special and she felt her lips lifting into a smile at his appearance. He was deliciously rumpled. She moved her hand to touch the back of his head. But he pulled away and climbed off her. He did up his trousers and put himself in order.

In the blink of an eye, something had changed between them and Clarry wasn't certain what it was. She sat up and hurried to cover up her legs.

Above her head, Lord Justin snorted. "There. Now you cannot claim I didn't make love to you."

CHAPTER FIVE

THAT MIGHT NOT HAVE BEEN the right thing to say immediately after the best sex of his life. But Justin felt so damn good about claiming Clarry in broad daylight that he hadn't thought to moderate his words. He still fumed over coming second to his brother. But at least his brother had never laid a finger, or anything else, on his future wife.

Clarry ignored him and stared at her clasped fingers.

After a long painful moment, Justin cleared his throat. "I should show you to your chamber and then fetch Miss Gainsford. My aunt will likely see to your needs. Be sure to consult her before approaching the duchess."

As Clarry nodded without looking up, Justin cursed himself for a fool. How could he expect that one moment of bliss could make any difference to his future?

He held out his hand to pull Clarry up, and eventually she placed her hand in his. Justin tugged her to her feet, cast a critical eye over her attire and deemed her ruined beyond all hope of repair. Well, there was no chance of correcting matters until they reached her new bedchamber. So, he tugged her against his side and led her out into the hallway.

Although the sensation of holding Clarry in his arms was pleasant, she sagged against him. He was literally carrying her by the time they reached her door. It hardly seemed the right time, they were not even married, yet Justin swung her up into his arms and carried her across the threshold.

Clarry was aware enough to gape at her surroundings. "Where are we?"

"Your new lodgings." Justin set her on the bed. "My bedchamber connects to this one though a sitting room."

Clarry swallowed, eyes wide in surprise. "I thought I was to be your mother's guest on the other side of the house. People will talk."

"They undoubtedly already are." Justin snatched her foot and removed her shoe. "But you will be at some liberty here in this part of the house. You should be comfortable."

Justin removed her other shoe and then set his hands to his hips. "It's been an eventful morning. Why don't you rest until Miss Gainsford arrives? Pull that bell when you awake and servants will bring you a bath, food and anything else you require."

Clarry slid from the bed as he turned away and followed him to the door. She tugged on his arm. "Where are you going after you visit with my father?"

Anywhere but here. He couldn't escape fast enough. "I shan't pester you again."

Although Clarry's mouth dropped open at his words, he didn't wait for her to speak. He turned the door handle to gain his freedom and slammed it closed behind him. The faint turning of a lock followed by a muffled sob came to him. Justin clenched his jaw tight as the sobs grew louder then eventually moved away from the door.

Well, what had she expected? Poetry and flowers after entrapping him into a marriage neither of them wanted. Justin's fury rose again and he stalked for the staircase. He'd take out his frustrations in the sparring room. The thickly padded floor muffled his steps as he crossed the spare chamber. He threw off his coat, waistcoat and even his shirt and cravat. He dragged off his boots so he stood barefoot before the punch bag. Justin danced up to it and swung a punch.

The solid thump gave him some satisfaction. So he hit again, and again, until a fine sheen of sweat broke out over his skin. The sting to his knuckles gave him some measure of peace and when they hurt enough, he grasped both sides of the pigskin bag and pressed his head against the leather while he caught his breath.

"Does that help, Jus?"

Justin turned his head until he could see the doorway. Tristan was leaning against the door jam. "Haven't you got better things to do, married man, than to pester other people?"

"Your happiness is important to me, brother. And you are not happy about this marriage. I can see only pain in your eyes. No happiness at all. What happened?" Tristan stepped further into the room and planted his feet as if he would never leave until he'd heard it all.

Justin slammed his fist into the bag again. Interfering bastard. The pain felt good so he kept hitting until Tristan caught his arm. "Justin?"

He shook off his brother's grip. "Mind your own damn business. You have a wife that loves you. Go back to her."

Tristan shook his head. "Not when you're

this upset. For God's sake, tell me what the problem is and we'll fix it."

"The problem." Justin threw his head back and laughed. "The problem is that my future wife mistook my bed for yours. We wouldn't be even getting married if you hadn't moved to the dower house." When his brother stared at him in confusion, Justin couldn't hold back. "She bloody well loves you, you moron. As usual, I'm second best. Not even *that* in her eyes."

Tristan's eyes widened. "But you love her? I know you do."

"Don't be ridiculous. She got into the wrong bed."

Tristan shook his head. "Justin, I know you loved Miss Wheaton before. I took great pains never to pay her any special attention. You know that."

"Well, it didn't work. She cried the whole way through the wedding and when she had enough liquid courage in her she slipped into your bed. Unfortunately, it turned out to be my bed and now I'm honor bound to marry her."

"Sweet Jesus. No wonder you're in a foul mood. What can I do to help?"

"Nothing." Justin turned on his brother. "Stay away from my future wife, stay away from us both. I'd rather not be reminded that I'm second best."

"Justin, you are not second best. She'll see that soon enough."

"Like our parents have?" Justin snorted. "That's my future, you see. For all this isn't an arranged marriage, she'll grow to dismiss me as father does mother's love."

"Your situation is as different as may be from that." Tristan caught both his arms and wouldn't let him go. "You can change Miss Wheaton's opinion of you. I know it. I dare you to at least try."

Justin shoved his brother back and glared. "Get out before I take my temper out on you."

Tristan held his hands up in defeat. "Fine. Fine. I'll inform mother we won't be joining you all at dinner this evening. Come and see me when you want to talk. My door is always open to you. Night or day, all right?"

Damn Tristan. He always knew the very thing to say to damp down Justin's anger. As Tristan walked out, Justin pressed the heel of his hands to his eyes. What an ugly mess his life had become. Because of his future wife's affections, he'd be denied his brother's company as well. Just when he would need him the most.

Justin strode up the front steps of Clarry's home and banged hard on the door. He ignored the neighbors peeking around their drapes or loitering in the street. Voices rose in anger from inside the Wheaton house so Justin banged again.

The voices quieted, and footsteps rushed toward the door. A red faced servant peeked around the wood. "Can I help you?"

Justin stood taller. "Lord Justin to see Mr. Wheaton if he has a moment to spare, that is?"

The butler smiled. "Do step in, my lord. I'll see if Mr. Wheaton is free."

The Wheaton drawing room was sparse but pleasant. Not as frilly as he imagined the room to be. He crossed to the hearth and stood with his back toward the fire, waiting for Mr. Wheaton to join him. The older man lumbered in moments later, and it was immediately apparent to Justin that Mr. Wheaton was deep in his cups already. His skin had flushed an angry red and his attire reminded him of a man after a night on the town.

Wheaton glared across the room. "What do you want now?"

"I've, ah, come to engage Miss Gainsford's services. I understand that she will likely be without a position now that Claribel is to be my wife."

"One woman ain't enough trouble for you now, huh? Gotta strip me of every bit o' feminine company. Well, ya cant av her. She's gone already."

"Already?" Somewhat stunned, Justin took a pace forward. "Did you dismiss her as soon as you returned?"

Mr. Wheaton ignored his approach and fell into a chair. "She flounced out of here on her own steam as soon as she heard what my fool daughter had done."

Justin didn't blame her, but he did worry. If Miss Gainsford had fled the house, she had likely had made a rash decision to do so. She might very well be regretting her decision at this moment. He'd better go be certain the woman understood she had a place to go if she needed one. "Ah, well then. I shouldn't trouble you any longer. Good day to you."

Mr. Wheaton grunted and Justin hurried out. On the stoop he paused to wonder where Miss Gainsford would go. He didn't have a clue, but he did know a place to start looking. He swung up on is horse and turned for town.

Devizes was bustling with activity this morning, and he felt every set of eyes turn to watch his passing. The townsfolk likely knew about his imminent marriage. They loved nothing better than to gossip, but he wasn't in the mood to fall into conversation with anyone. He swung off his horse at the lending library, the one place everyone seemed to gravitate too, and crooked a finger at the blacksmith's boy loitering along the street.

As the boy took the reins, Justin headed inside the lending library, looking for his new sister-in-law's father. Mr. Charles Davey peeked around the corner and scowled. "Oh, it's you. What are you after here?"

"I've come in search of Miss Wheaton's companion. A woman by the name of Miss Bethany Gainsford. I've called at the Wheaton residence and was informed that she'd left service there. My future wife would like her to continue in her role as companion."

Although such a long explanation was hardly necessary, Justin believed he would get more help by being completely honest.

The older man snorted. "Miss Wheaton wants her, you say?"

"Yes, she was afraid her father would turn her out without references. She appears quite right to be concerned."

Soft footfalls approached from the rear of the building and a young woman appeared. "Miss Gainsford? I am relieved to find you so quickly. I take it you overheard my conversation with Mr. Davey?"

The other woman nodded, but she seemed wary. "Where is Miss Wheaton?"

Justin hoped his smile encouraged her lagging spirit. "The duchess has invited her to stay at Staplehurst Hall but she was most concerned for your welfare. We would like you to continue in your position as her companion."

"No, thank you."

Justin nodded. "We can be on our way as soon as you are ready."

The little woman looked at him quizzically. "Did you not hear me correctly, my lord? I decline to remain with Miss Wheaton as her companion. I am quite capable of taking care of myself."

Well, this was quite unlike how he'd expected this to end. As if another disappointment should have surprised him today. "Where will you go?"

Her gaze fixed on Mr. Davey. "I secured a position as housekeeper for Mr. Davey, my lord. I have a roof over my head and a vastly improved position in terms of my duties."

A housekeeper was a vast step down from that of companion, and the work was considerably more exhausting. Was she addled? Justin felt compelled to give the girl one more chance. "Are you sure? Life at the Hall would be a vast deal easier."

Mr. Davey chuckled. "Tried to change her mind myself. But she seems concerned I'm on the brink of starvation. But I do need a house-keeper now that my daughter has married. Be-sides, Miss Gainsford has a fine mind. She may read through the library as time allows."

Ah. That boon would not come with the position as companion at the Hall. "As you wish, Miss Gainsford, but should you change your mind please come to the Hall."

"I'll not need to," Miss Gainsford insisted.

Seeing that he had come on a fool's errand, Justin took his leave, collected his horse and turned for Staplehurst Hall. His path today mir-rored yesterday's trip after the wedding, but his mood now was even grimmer. How could he survive a marriage to Clarry when she had no love for him?

The lust he'd roused in her this morning and last night would fade, as all lust surely did until he was the only one clinging to the memory of what might have been. He shook his head to clear his maudlin thoughts. When they were married, he'd return to his work, his second love of writing, and devote himself wholeheartedly to making peace with his soul.

As he left his horse with a groom, he won-dered what Clarry would say about losing her companion. He hadn't known they were particularly close until this morning when she had seemed genuinely concerned for Miss Gainsford's wellbeing. Yet, Miss Gainsford had no wish to be reunited with her charge. Interesting. But not enough to lift the dark cloud hovering over his head.

Justin strode through the Hall and ignored that the staff quickly looked elsewhere. They would already have combined the events of last night, with the evidence found in his bedchamber this morning. They would know he'd been caught fair and square for seducing a virgin. The smear of blood upon his sheets was damning proof of his guilt.

Justin stopped. Christ, how could he have bedded a woman and not realized her true innocence. He'd thought the hesitation was part of Lucy's game, but the truth was he'd taken something more important. The night should have been a profoundly moving experience for Claribel.

Justin crossed to a window and stared out at the perfectly clipped grounds. She must think him a beast, a brute that forced himself upon her. Justin banged his forehead against the wood frame. Idiot. And then to compound the problem he'd taken her so swiftly on the sofa in a guest room. She had every right to hate him.

He should have noticed the difference last

night. He should have recognized Clarry in the dark. Bothered that he hadn't, he reluctantly continued on. He would check on her and if she was awake he would apologize and promise to stay away. It was the least he could do. His bedchamber was free of servants when he entered and he poured himself a large brandy.

As the glass reached his lips, voices drifted to him from the adjoining sitting room. Puzzled, he crept to the doorway and listened.

"Now turn around and do that again."

The Duchess. Justin set his hand to the door knob and turned it slowly. The door opened with nary a sound and he pressed his eye to the crack. Inside, he found his mother and aunt and a very tired looking Clarry, walking up and down the sitting room carpet. What the hell were they up to?

He opened the door wider. As far as he could tell at first glance, there was nothing different about Clarry. But then he noticed how high her breasts rose in her gown and the tiny breaths she took. Justin had a good memory of her endowments but she usually did not flaunt them like that. He stepped through the doorway and cleared his throat to get their attention, surprising everyone including himself.

"Justin, my dear, you shouldn't be here," his mother protested.

Justin scowled. "Neither should you. I left instructions that Clarry was not to be disturbed for any reason until she called for the servants. Since she appears as fatigued as when I left, I can only conclude someone disobeyed me."

"Well," the duchess huffed indignantly. "I do my best to help and this is the thanks I get." The duchess gathered her things and stormed out. His aunt's shoulders drooped in relief and she cast an apologetic glance at Clarry then followed her sister.

Justin locked the door after them and turned to face his future wife. "Did you sleep at all?" he asked softly.

A sigh escaped Clarry. "A little. But it is very hard to ignore the duchess when she is standing over your bed."

"Forgive me. I had not thought she would seek you out."

Clarry's color rose to a bright pink abruptly. Concerned that she might faint from a lack of air, Justin led Clarry back to her bedchamber and toward her bed. He stripped the gown from her body then went to work loosening the corset strings. When he'd half undone the corset, Clarry pulled a gasping breath deep into her lungs.

He stroked his fingers over her exposed skin. "Better?"

"Much better, thank you."

Since he received no discouragement, Justin continued to touch. "I shall try to prevent her from inflicting such torture on you again. I'll burn all your corsets if necessary."

A tired laugh escaped her. "Burning is not necessary. But I'd prefer to draw in a full breath if I could."

Since Clarry had not yet realized that she stood half naked in his presence, Justin pulled her into his arms. She didn't resist; she sagged into his embrace with a soft sigh. He set his lips to her throat and pressed soft kisses to her skin. A pleased purr rumbled from her and he glanced at her face anxiously. Clarry stood with her eyes closed, lips parted, face slack. She appeared so sleepy that Justin flushed with chagrin. He should exert a little more effort to care for her if he wished to make this marriage bearable for each of them. Hadn't he intended not to bother her moments before?

The task might be more difficult than he imagined, but he would do what he could to make this marriage easy for her. Without peeking too much he removed her corset, scooped her up into his arms and tucked her into bed.

Confused, languid eyes blinked up at him. "Do you want to make love again?"

Justin's skin pricked with heat at her question. He would love nothing more than to please her, but he had never been what she wanted. He brushed a lock of hair away from her eyes gently. She was so very beautiful. Despite the circumstances, Justin didn't deserve her. "No, I'm going to see to it that you sleep undisturbed."

Clarry curled into a ball, her eyes fluttered shut. "A pity. I could become used to making love."

CHAPTER SIX

CLARRY LEANED against her new bed and
stared into the flames leaping in the hearth.
What a ghastly day, and what a nightmare
dinner had been with the duke and duchess
tonight. She'd never felt more uncomfortable in
her life. She crawled into bed and opened her
book, hoping to block out her situation. Perhaps
she could become lost in a different reality for
just a bit.

Words of love, devotion and yearning filled
every page and her heart soared as she read the
well-loved lines of her favorite book of romantic
poetry. To be treasured like this was a dream.
No man, living or dead could ever feel for her
what this anonymous poet had felt for his lady
love.

She traced her fingers over the bold letters,

penned so carefully and each page embellished with flowers. It was a lucky day for Clarry to have found this treasure, and even luckier that the small tome had been included with her belongings when her father had sent them to Staplehurst Hall.

He had no use for poetry, or music or even words. The long silences at home were unnerving at times but she'd done her best to find excuses to be from home as often as she could. Clarry closed the book and set it beneath the pillow, where she kept it every night. She'd never be loved like that.

The chamber around her was filled with deep shadows, and the Hall beyond her door had settled down for the night. But Clarry was restless after her brush with the duchess. Her Grace quite clearly disapproved of her, and disapproved of Justin's plan to marry her. Her displeasure had centered on Clarry, not Justin. It seemed she was to marry the duchess's favorite son.

Clarry had thought Lord Ramsbury, heir to the great estate around her, would have been the one the duchess favored. But she seemed inordinately fond of her youngest son, and had thrown daggers with her eyes at Clarry whenever Lord Justin had been otherwise engaged in conversation. Only the occasional brush of his hand across her leg beneath the table had bolstered her flagging spirits.

She reminded herself constantly that he was the one she had to learn to live with.

She leaned back and closed her eyes. She'd been such a stupid fool to risk her reputation, to place her faith in the words of a servant about who slept where within this house. Poor Lord Justin, he must be furious with her entrapment. Yet there had been few occasions where she'd sensed true anger. After his initial reaction in his bedchamber, he'd seemed more disappointed with the turn of his life than angry.

Well, that would have to change. Although she'd made a less than admirable start with him, Clarry would be his wife and she should make an attempt to please him. Her mother had never managed it for her father, he'd remained critical of everything while her mother was around, but Clarry was made of stronger mettle than her mother. She didn't want that kind of life for herself so she'd try to be exactly what Lord Justin wanted for a wife.

But what did she know of Lord Justin?

He was tall, smiled foolishly a lot, and was something of a writer, according to his mother and aunt. He was rather attractive with his wavy brown hair and wide hazel eyes, and he did dress rather splendidly, given he was only a spare. Lord Justin and his brother, Lord Ramsbury, were very different creatures, though, which was why she'd fallen in love with Lord Ramsbury in the first place. When Ramsbury spoke, people listened. Ramsbury generously included those around him, no matter their rank.

Lord Justin? Well, he was quieter and had visited Devizes infrequently in the past year so she was a little uncertain about his character. What she knew of him came mostly from gossip. In fact, they had hardly spoken in the last year. Clarry snuggled further into the bed as she remembered the afternoon, Lord Justin's arms wrapped tightly about her body. A tremor ran through her. Perhaps if she encouraged his more amorous inclinations they might make a better go of this marriage. He did make her feel wonderful when they made love.

A floorboard creaked and Clarry started, finding Lord Justin inches from the bed.

She pressed her hand over her heart. "Oh, my lord, you scared me."

Lord Justin stood straighter. "Forgive me. I thought you had fallen asleep and neglected to snuff the candle. I was merely intending to put it out."

Clarry sat up, tucking the covers tightly

around her to ward off the chill. "No, not sleeping. I was thinking about today."

"Do you mean dinner with my mother and aunt?" He scowled. "We've had words already."

Aghast to be the source of further discord, Clarry leaned forward to capture Lord Justin's arm. "The duchess has every right to be angry with me. I should never have behaved so foolishly. I am very sorry for the situation we now find ourselves in."

As her hand slid down his arm, he captured her fingers in a loose grip. "So you regret attempting to seduce a married man?"

"Well, yes, of course I do. I don't know what I was thinking. I am sorry to have dragged you into this mess."

"Not a total mess." A sudden grin crossed his face then disappeared. "There are some parts of this arrangement that are pleasant."

Clarry's face heated. He was talking about making love. Well, at least she managed to do something right with him. Lord Justin's eyes dropped low, skimming over the skin of her chest revealed by her loose night gown. The garment was light and comfortable to wear, but also revealed a little more skin than she'd remembered. Lord Justin didn't appear offended by her state. He leaned forward, brushed her hair over her shoulder, and pressed his lips to the base of her throat.

Clarry closed her eyes to savor the sensations. He used his mouth very well, and not just for talking. A small moan left her mouth as he propelled her backwards until she lay flat on the bed again. When she opened her eyes, Lord Justin hovered above, both hands pressed to the mattress on either side of her shoulders. His face creased into a roguish smile then he swooped low to kiss her properly. Oh yes, he made her feel wonderful. She set her hands to his waist and pulled him closer.

"Clarry," he whispered against her parted lips. "Send me out of the room."

"Well, you're here and I'm here. It's not as if we haven't done this before."

Justin groaned against her throat. "You can refuse me. You *do* know that, don't you?"

She caught a glimpse of the troubled expression on his face and set her hand to his cheek. "I probably shall one day, but not tonight. I want to please you."

Justin's cheek settled beside hers. The harsh rush of his breath delighting her senses, the light stubble of his jaw scraped across her skin. "It is a hollow coupling when only one gains pleasure from the encounter, Clarry. You should be satisfied as well."

Clarry swallowed hard. Had what they'd shared not been enough for him? "Do you mean there is more to making love?"

"Making love is like poetry. The experience is better when shared."

"And I've displeased you in bed?" How utterly humiliating. Clarry scrambled out from under Lord Justin and hugged her arms about her chest.

Lord Justin, however, caught her ankle and dragged her back until she laid trapped half beneath him. "I'd hardly say I'm displeased. I was more concerned for you. You should not feel like you must allow me further liberties before we marry. I would not have you resent me for..."

When he didn't finish, Clarry finished for him. "For taking my innocence, even if I threw myself into your bed."

Lord Justin evaded her gaze. "Something like that."

"From where I'm sitting, you've been very good to me. Making love is not at all what I had heard of the experience. I could stand to make love to you again if you wanted that."

Lord Justin's features altered until a foolish grin broke across his face. When he smiled like that he was quite adorable so she leaned forward to capture his lips. The first brush was softened by Justin lifting his head. He stared into her eyes as they kissed, his fingers slid along her arm and her skin prickled with gooseflesh. Her breath caught as he eased onto the bed at her side. His toes touched hers, rubbing gently over her colder ones.

He shifted again until they were eye to eye, her knees pressed against his thighs. When he was standing, he was so tall she feared she would strain her neck. But in this position, they were equals, and each breathing as hard as the other. Clarry lifted her hand to his cheek and brushed her fingertips across his skin, stopping when she reached his jaw, and then sliding her thumb across the rough surface to his ear.

His hand covered her breast and Clarry bit her lip to hold back a moan. How had he turned her into such a desirous lady in so short a length of time? His thumb stroked her nipple as she brushed the edge of his ear. She rolled nearer to him, eager to feel his warmth against her body.

They kissed, softly at first but as Clarry snuggled against the hardness of his chest, their tongues danced with more passion.

Justin pulled away first. "Too many clothes between us," he muttered.

He stripped himself, then caught up the bottom of her night gown and tugged it over her head. Clarry blushed. They were both very naked. No one had warned her about this aspect of male and female relations.

If Clarry hadn't been lying down, she may have swooned. Justin was a fine specimen of male anatomy, and he was coming closer. He slid into bed beside her and rested his head on his hand. With him leaning over her the way he was, it was as if nothing else existed in the world but them.

Again, his fingertips drifted over her skin, raising gooseflesh on every part. His lips curled up in a soft smile as Clarry strove to remain still. He tickled her ever so slightly at her waist and she flinched. Her hip brushed his manhood and a moan erupted from Justin's mouth. Astonished by his reaction, Clarry rolled to her side and studied him.

His wide muscled chest rose and fell rapidly. She set her hand to it, sliding her fingers gently over his skin the way he had her. He seemed to like the caress because his eyes drifted shut. He was warm under her hand and she drew that warmth, and the scent of him, deep into her. She touched his waist, then his hips, and lowered her eyes to look at what else there was of him.

His manhood was full, rigid between them. Clarry hesitated a bare moment before sliding her hand until her fingertips rested on the length. The soft touch caused Justin to gasp. His manhood jumped and returned to rest against her fingers. Clarry smiled. He was as sensitive as she perhaps. His light caress had been utter torture.

She did not want to torture him. She wanted to make him happy, so she curled her fingers around his length and held him.

"Damn, that feels so good," he groaned.

Clarry preened. She had made him happy with her boldness, and she would keep him that way. She squeezed a little harder and then eased her grip. Justin covered her hand and moved it up and down his length.

When he released her, she mimicked his movement, fascinated by the strength beneath his skin and the rasp of his breath against her hair. Moisture beaded at the tip and she frowned at it. Should it be there? Should she do something about it before it dripped?

On an upward stroke, Clarry brushed her thumb over the moisture, rubbing it into the tip. Justin's loud groan filled the chamber. He grabbed her leg, dragged it over his thigh and pressed his hand between her spread legs and covered her womanly parts.

Clarry sucked in a startled breath at the sensation. He parted her lower lips with his fingers and set a thousand nerves alight. She bit her lip, striving to ignore what he was doing and continue to stoke him.

But Justin knew what he was about better than Clarry did. He brought her to that magical place quickly with very little effort. Her hips rolled against his hand, almost as if they had a life of their own. She squeezed Justin as he pushed her into the ultimate pleasure. She wailed and clenched his hand with her thighs.

Justin moaned too and warmth spread over her belly. She looked down in time to see another spurt leave his manhood and paint her belly with his seed. She blushed. So that was what happened to him when they made love?

She met his gaze and saw the high color of his cheeks, the dazed look in his eyes and grinned. He'd come undone, exactly as he made her feel by the look of it.

He pressed his head to hers and closed his eyes. "Are you all right?"

What a ridiculous question. "Of course. That was wonderful."

He muttered something under his breath as he climbed out of bed. He crossed the room to the wash basin, dampened a wash cloth and returned. "Sorry. This will likely be cold."

Clarry flinched as the cold cloth touched her stomach and Justin thoroughly cleansed her skin. He patted her with a dry length of cloth, covered her with the counterpane, and moved back.

"Where are you going?"

"To my bed."

Clarry's heart hammered, astonishing her in the process. She didn't want to be alone tonight. She didn't want Justin to leave. She swallowed the lump forming in her throat. "If you must."

"Well"—Justin rocked on his heels—"good night then."

Curse it all, he really was going to go. What had she expected? He'd got what he wanted from her—pleasure. Now he would leave her to think about her wanton behavior all night. Her skin heated in embarrassment, as she tried to reconcile herself to this pattern of her future life. "Good night, my lord. Pleasant dreams."

Her voice shook on the last words. Their eyes met. Justin took a pace forward. "Are you really all right?"

Clarry raised a hand to her cheek and pressed against the burning hot flesh. "Just a little overwhelmed. I'm sure I'll grow used to things in time."

"It must be strange to be in a new place, and under such circumstances. I don't have to leave. I can stay if you'd prefer to have my company during the night. I'll be sure to leave early before the servants come."

Clarry sighed as relief rushed through her. She crooked her fingers at Lord Justin. "Come back to bed."

CHAPTER SEVEN

AS MUCH AS Justin would like to spend the day in bed with his future wife he couldn't risk it. When Clarry woke, she'd have come to her senses and he couldn't bear the thought of hearing from her own lips that last night was a mistake. He eased to the side of the bed carefully, listening to her breathing change as she rolled onto her side, and then fall asleep again. He slid out of Clarry's rumpled sheets, collected up his scattered clothes, and crept from the room without looking back. He didn't want the servants to find him there at this hour. They had more than enough gossip to dissect from the first night they'd slept together. Any more and they would never live down the scandal.

He stopped in the adjoining sitting room and tugged on his drawers and shirt. Making love to Clarry, when she didn't love him in return, would break his heart. She may appear to enjoy making love to him but when she closed her eyes she'd be thinking of his brother. Afterwards, holding her in his arms last night while she slept, had been heaven until morning brought the stark reminder that he couldn't keep her away from the man she loved forever.

Eventually, she would see Tristan and her expression would shift until she resembled a small, affection-starved puppy. And Justin would have to stand back and watch the whole ghastly disappointment play out over Clarry's face and pretend it didn't bother him. He hoped he was strong enough not to resent his brother for the mess he was in. It was hardly Tristan's fault he was universally adored.

Justin headed for his bedchamber. He'd make a show of rumpling his bed before the servants were about to allay any gossip about where he'd spent the night. But, as he crossed the room, he spied a body in his bed and drew to a halt. Justin skirted the sleeping form cautiously. What the devil was Lucy doing tucked up in his bed and sound asleep?

He glanced behind him anxiously and then reminded himself that Clarry probably wouldn't care who he appeared to sleep with. Unfortunately, Justin did. He didn't want anyone to think he'd be an unfaithful man even before his wedding day. He set his hand to Lucy's shoulder and gently shook her awake.

A kittenish whimper left Lucy's lips as she blinked up at him. Then her face creased into a contented smile. "There you are, my lord."

"What are you doing here?"

"Waiting for you. I thought you'd forgotten about me, but I'm glad I waited. Come to bed?"

Justin recoiled from her suggestion and for good measure, clasped his hands behind his back so she couldn't pull him into bed with her. He didn't want what Lucy offered anymore. Now he had Clarry as his wife he would give up chasing any other skirts but hers. "I hadn't expected to find you in my bed, Lucy. You should not be here."

Her eyes flickered over his disheveled appearance and her gaze narrowed. "So the rumors are quite true. You're actually bedding the little mouse?"

How dare she speak of Clarry in such a disparaging fashion? At least she didn't spread her legs for any gentlemen with coin the way Lucy did. Justin stepped forward. "What I do or do not do is hardly your affair. I suggest you remember exactly what your place is, Lucy. You are speaking of my future wife."

"But you always encourage me to speak my mind, especially when I'm in your bed." Lucy patted the mattress and sat up. Her unbound hair hung in waves about her shoulders. The upper swells of her bosom exposed from the loosened confines of her bodice as she toyed with the edge of her dress. "I can make you forget her."

Justin shook his head. There wasn't a day that passed when he didn't think about what Clarry might be up to. Lucy had, until now, merely diverted his mind for a few pleasurable minutes. "I did not invite you to my bed last night," Justin cast a hasty glance toward his future wife's chamber, praying the sound of their conversation didn't travel far.

The brazen flirt slid from the sheets and sauntered forward, adding a saucy sway to her hips. "But you did the night before and I simply had to make it up to you. I'm sure that little mouse is as boring in bed as she's rumored to be out of it."

Lucy's triumphant expression angered him. Justin grasped Lucy by the arm and towed her toward the door. "There will be no more invitations. Do not return here again."

The little oomph Lucy expelled as he tossed her from the room lasted but a moment as she collided with his friend, Roderick Ford's, chest.

Lucy let out a delighted squeal and wrapped herself around Roddy. "You're back!"

As far as old friends went, Roddy was Justin's oldest London acquaintance. They had similar backgrounds: both born second sons, both frequently short of funds. There was no end of topics that they could lament over while sharing a drink or a woman.

"Justin, I never truly appreciated until now how generous you are with your females." Roddy pulled Lucy's arms from his neck. "Come see me later, wench. If Lord Justin has no further need of your delightful services, I'm more than happy to become reacquainted with your charms."

"It will be my pleasure." She smiled broadly, turned and sauntered down the hall. The exaggerated sway of her hips kept Roddy's attention until she disappeared from sight.

"That's one hell of a girl you have there."

"She's yours now."

Roddy chuckled. "Well, she will be shortly."

Justin supposed he should be grateful for the distraction but he wasn't in the mood to listen to them discuss their bed play in the hall. He grabbed his friends arm and dragged him into his bedchamber then shut the door. "What the hell are you doing back here again?"

"Heard your older brother had settled on a wife and since I happened to be in the area I thought to pay my respects." He glanced at the unmade bed. "Your mother made the most delightful invitation to make myself at home but I see I should have delayed my arrival just a little longer. Did I interrupt?"

"There was nothing to interrupt in the first place. Lucy was just passing by." Justin raked his fingers through his hair. "How are you, Roddy?"

"Fine. Fine. But all this talk of wedded bliss is making my feet itch. Ghastly nonsense. When are you headed back to Town? I thought we might travel together."

Justin winced. "I'll not be back to town for a while actually. I have business here in Wiltshire."

Roddy settled on Justin's rumpled bed and set his hands behind his head. "Oh, what mad scheme have you latched onto now? Have you found another race horse to buy?"

"Actually, I'm to marry, too."

The silence lasted a bare second.

Roddy leapt to his feet. "Well, bugger me. It seems I've come at a precipitous moment. I've always said fate leads you where you should go. You do remember our bet don't you?"

Oh, hell. Justin swallowed. "Surely you cannot still mean to go through with it."

Roddy glanced around eagerly. "A bet is a

bet, Justin. I must say, I'm glad you're the one to fall on their sword first over this. Hand it over. Victory is mine."

"Oh, come on. That bet should never have been made. It's hardly decent."

Roddy rubbed his hands together briskly. "I'll write to Norris and have him post the notice in the club. I think scheduling a recital of your poetry Friday next will be ample warning for those interested parties wanting to attend."

Justin raked his hand through his hair. "I don't have the journal."

"I don't believe that for a minute!" Roddy turned for the writing desk and rummaged through the loose papers. "I've waited five long years to see your scribbling. You're never without the ruddy thing tucked under your arm."

Justin pushed Roddy away from the desk and straightened the papers. "I lost the book months ago. It's gone."

Roddy grabbed his arm and forced Justin to look at him. "Then I believe you know what else you have to hand over to me before the wedding."

He couldn't. "Roddy, really, you cannot possibly expect—"

"Ah, but those were the terms, old man. The first to marry either suffers public humiliation at the club or a private humiliation before his future wife. I'm so looking forward to spending time alone with her. I told you I wouldn't forget. Who is she?"

Justin raked his fingers through his hair. How the hell had circumstances lined up to further ruin his chances for happiness. Clarry would never speak to him again once she learned of his foolishness. "Someone too good for either of us. But since you are so keen to be a bastard, I shall be sure to collect my side of the bargain as well when the time comes. I'm sure the world would like to know why Lady Beth disappeared from good society."

Roddy's jaw clenched tight. "Now see here. It was first to marry who suffered the humiliation."

"That's not how I remember it. And a great pity the terms were never recorded at our club. So here is fair warning. I won't be satisfied with private humiliation. I value my future wife far too much to seek a glimpse of yours naked. But I will expose your hand in Lady Beth's fall from grace if you attempt to claim your winnings from my bride. Lord Monteford must be getting anxious to get his daughter back."

"The scandal will kill him," Roddy whispered. "He has a weak heart."

"It wasn't me who led that girl astray. You

led her on while pursuing an empty-headed heiress, and then married neither of them. No wonder she ran away from the humiliation."

Roddy's hands clenched. "You don't know what happened. But you'll ruin us all if you speak of the matter."

Justin's fingers curled into fists. "And you will ruin my wife's reputation when word of your private tête-à-tête gets out."

Roddy's jaw clenched. "It hardly seems you care too much about the woman given I caught you with the luscious Lucy in your bed this morning."

"Lucy misunderstood an earlier conversation and I was just explaining the error of her ways. An invitation to her will never pass my lips again." When Roddy smirked, Justin stepped forward. "This isn't a laughing matter. Breathe one word to my future wife and we cease to be friends, Roddy."

Roddy took a pace back. "So you were in bed alone? That's not what it looks like."

"I didn't sleep with Lucy last night." He watched his friend carefully. Roddy would eventually discover Clarry's bedchamber lay close to his. But he didn't want him to know now before the pair had actually met.

"Well, I see you're not in much of a talking mood. Perhaps later you can introduce me to your betrothed so we might become better acquainted." Roddy tossed off a laugh as he headed out the door.

As the door closed Justin cursed. Damn it. He did not need Roddy here at a time like this. Not when the scandal of their hasty marriage remained fresh in everyone's mind. Roddy would make him the laughing stock of their club within an hour of returning to London. Not for the first time did Justin wonder why they remained friends. Perhaps shared secrets had bound them together, but now perhaps he should drop the acquaintance. Clarry would undoubtedly find it impossible to meet with Roddy again after this.

Justin collapsed onto his bed and rolled over to bury his face in his pillow. Blast it all. He'd always thought his eventual marriage wouldn't start out well, but he'd never imagined these poor circumstances.

Clarry recoiled from the door in horror. What kind of man had she tied herself to? He debauched servants, had no sense when it came to horses, and worst of all had wagered away her reputation before he'd even married her. She set her hands to her stomach and tried to think. The situation had gone too far to get out of the marriage. Running away wouldn't accomplish anything but distress. She doubted Lord Justin would care if she disappeared. And the thought of submitting to a stranger the way she had to Lord Justin turned her stomach.

There had to be a way to ruin the bet. There had to. Clarry spun about and then gasped. The duchess. Dear God, how long had she been standing there?

Her Grace's brow rose haughtily. "Its all rather ghastly, isn't it?"

"Your Grace." Clarry fumbled an awkward curtsey. But the duchess caught her elbow and dragged her to her bedchamber.

Clarry couldn't tolerate another dressing session with Justin's mother so she turned about and set her hands to her hips. "Can I help you, Your Grace?"

The duchess tapped her finger against her pursed lips. The sudden smile that followed sent a chill racing through her. "No. But perhaps I can help you."

Clarry held the older woman's gaze, trying to decide just how the duchess could help. Was she offering to let her escape the wedding?

The duchess settled herself into a chair. "I take it by your expression you did not enjoy the conversation conducted in my son's bed chamber."

Clarry nodded, but had to ask, "Which part did you overhear?"

"All of the essentials, I imagine. My son must either stand up and read his poetry to a bunch of wastrels with no appreciation for his art, or you must submit to the dubious honor of spending time alone in Lord Roderick's company before the wedding. Neither one will please my son. But which form of torture appeals to you?"

"Neither. I'm not acquainted with Lord Roderick."

The duchess shook her head. "Not worth the acquaintance in my opinion. But Justin is loyal to those he cares for, even in the face of thoroughly reprehensible behavior. I wonder what he knows of Lady Beth?"

Clarry shook her head. She didn't know who this Lady Beth was but the outcome of whatever had happened didn't sound good. She hoped the duchess wouldn't suggest she acquire more information directly from Lord Justin. She didn't believe sharing would be high on his list of priorities just yet.

"Well, no matter. We'll get to the bottom of that mess eventually but well after you have shackled my son in matrimony. I'm expecting the duke to return tomorrow or the day after."

Clarry gulped. "So soon."

The duchess leaned sideways in her chair to look around her. "Not soon enough if that's how your bed shall look every morning until the wedding actually happens. You could at least make it appear as if you slept alone. Straighten the bed up a bit, girl, before a servant arrives."

Clarry whirled about and fumbled with the sheets.

The duchess's sigh reached her ears. "The servant, Lucy, will be removed to another of our properties today. I will not allow her to cause discord in my son's marriage before it even starts."

Clarry set her hands to the mattress where Lord Justin had laid last night and breathed a sigh of intense relief. It surprised her that she might care where her future husband spent his nights, but she was relieved not to have to run into the servant about the Hall. "Thank you."

Her Grace chuckled quite wickedly and Clarry spun about. "I don't know if you should thank me just yet, given the circumstances that brought about this union. It's very likely I'm condemning you to spending all your nights entertaining my son."

Clarry hurried to smooth the comforter in place. "That is a husbands right, isn't it?"

The duchess crossed the room and captured her arm. "Never, ever, let me hear you say that again out loud. You have every right to refuse Justin. You must make a place for yourself at his side, not three steps behind as if you were his servant to be used and discarded when you lost your figure. Did your mother's flight from the district and your father's temper not teach you anything?"

What she thought of her mother was hardly an opinion Clarry expected the duchess to appreciate. She'd thought obeying the duchess's son would be one of the strictures. Should she mention she thought her mother lucky to have gone? Clarry licked her lips. "I hardly remember her."

The duchess pursed her lips, and then they stretched into a knowing smile. "I think you remember more than you let on. Very well, meet me in the green salon directly after you've broken your fast. Perhaps you'll do after all."

The duchess chuckled and swept from the chamber, leaving Clarry more confused than ever.

CHAPTER EIGHT

DAMN IT. Where the hell was she? Justin had scoured the Hall from top to bottom and had failed to find his future bride. Had she absconded as her father claimed she might or had his mother removed her without warning? Mother had taken no pains to hide her disapproval of the match. Would she go as far as send Clarry away while his back was turned? He hoped not because as far as he was concerned, Clarry was already his wife. The ceremony—a necessary formality.

He paced Clarry's chamber, noting her possessions still remained strewn around the room. Her tortoiseshell hairbrush and combs remained exactly where she'd dropped them. He picked one up and turned it over in his hands, then tugged out loose strands of her hair from the bristles.

He missed her.

What a total idiot he'd become. They'd been apart merely a half day and he longed to see her happy still. Acting the part of a love-sick swain came easily to him. After all, he'd loved Clarry for years, even if she'd ignored him. Justin set the comb aside carefully and forced himself to sit and wait. But patience had never been his strong suit.

Restless, he adjusted the cushions, until his hand bumped something solid. He pulled out a book and sat it on his lap. But the stunning sight of it took his breath away. This was his book. *Lightning strike him*—his journal. The one he'd lost months ago and searched for in every place imaginable.

How on earth had it come into Clarry's possession?

The doorknob turned and Justin shoved the book beneath the pillow again.

"Oh, Lord Justin, I wasn't expecting you. Did you want something?"

Nervously, Justin stood up and faced his future wife. His tongue thickened in his throat. What did she think of his poetry? Every word penned into that book had been written about her and he wondered if she knew he was the author. Did she recognize herself in those pages? "I, ah, just wanted, to, ah, see if you were well."

She frowned at him and set her bonnet on a table. "Perfectly well. I've just been to call on Lady Ramsbury with your aunt and mother."

Justin scowled. "You saw my brother?"

"No." Did her voice tremble? "Just the viscountess. Your mother and aunt insisted I pay a social call with them. They are beside themselves about the baby. I hadn't heard a whisper that your sister-in-law was with child."

Justin watched Clarry to see how she felt about the news. In all honesty, he couldn't gauge her reaction. "We learned of it the day he proposed."

Clarry sighed and settled into the space he'd just vacated. "A month ago."

The words were spoken in such a hollow tone that Justin winced for her pain. He stared down at the top of her head and wondered what she was thinking. From this angle, he couldn't see her face well enough to judge whether she was desperately unhappy. He sat close to her side and slid his hand over her clenched fingers. "From what I understand my aunt suspected first. And I knew Tristan had his eye on a woman here. I just couldn't figure out whom though. He managed to keep Win a secret, even from me."

"You liked her." Clarry's words rang with accusation. "You were often in her company."

Startled by her reaction, he squeezed her hand. "I'm human, and she is very lovely. But she's Tristan's wife now, my new sister, and she's very much in love with him. They suit each other."

Clarry nodded then pressed her hand to her temple.

"Are you all right?" He changed his grip and laced their fingers together as naturally as if they were long time lovers.

Clarry shook her head. "I am such a fool not to have suspected how deep their attachment went. I thought if I could just get him alone he would see me differently. See the real me. But I messed that up and now we're saddled with each other."

Justin dropped her hand and stood. "Perhaps you'll grow used to marriage and me in time. I will see you at dinner."

"Wait. I didn't mean it to come out that way. I'm just saying that you wouldn't be in this situation if I'd had all the facts. You'd never have chosen to court me in the first place, let alone offer marriage, if I hadn't ruined myself."

Justin stood still. Should he tell her the truth before the wedding or hold his heart close to his chest to protect himself. Yet if he didn't express his feelings soon he feared he'd burst out with his love at an inopportune time, such as while making love. And that he couldn't bear because he wouldn't hear the same sentiments returned. "I would have courted you properly for the whole world to see if you had smiled at me with half the strength with which you do my brother. I envied him, and it's hardly a secret that you preferred him and his title."

A lengthy silence followed her short gasp and with no attempt at denial Justin returned to his bedchamber without glancing at Clarry's face.

Clarry sat very still and willed her heart to slow. Had she just imagined that Justin might once have had honorable intentions toward her? That couldn't be right. She must have misheard him. He preferred tall women, elegant creatures who'd already had a husband. At least that's what she'd heard whispered about town often enough. Even Lady Ramsbury fit his type of lover. Whereas Clarry, at five feet two and more flesh on her bones than she cared for, couldn't be more different. Yet he sounded a jealous man.

Curious, Clarry crept toward the doorway adjoining her room to Justin's sitting room. All was quiet. Still. So she quickly crossed the room and peeked into his bedchamber. Empty. Dash it all. Now she might never know. As she turned to cross the room she spied his writing desk. The surface was buried under scraps of parchment, strewn every which way about. She straightened a few before one caught her eye.

Her eyes glow hot as embers
    Her touch burns my soul
    Yet for a taste of her cherry red lips
    ~~A man would walk through hell~~

Thankfully the last line had been crossed out. How terribly mundane. Clarry read another and as she reached the last line she realized something important. Justin's handwriting seemed familiar. The loops and swirls pricked her memory. They reminded her of —

Her book!

But that couldn't be possible. Her poet had music in his soul and a greater love in his heart than Lord Justin ever could. The writing must only be similar in style. But still the feel of it was too familiar to ignore. Perhaps he knew the writer well. Yes, that was it. He must have fashioned his own poetry after someone else. It happened all the time. To prove her point she snatched up a sheet, returned to her chamber, and picked up the small pillow on the chaise. The journal of poetry wasn't there. Clarry frantically searched and let out a relieved breath when she found it at the other end of the chaise.

Her heart stilled. She always sat on the right side of the couch, the journal tucked under the little scatter cushions so it couldn't be stumbled upon. She'd never leave it closer to the door. When she remembered Justin had awaited her return on this couch recently her heart tumbled over. Had he read the journal while he waited? Read it then hidden it in the wrong place?

Now that she thought of it he had seemed uncomfortable. Did he dislike her reading another man's pretty words? Idly, Clarry flipped open the book and compared the handwriting. The journal's lettering flowed neatly across the page, but the scrap of paper in her hand contained a messy scrawl. As she peered at them in turn she did detect similarities. The looping y's ended with the same flourish. The a's and e's matching in height and size.

Clarry frowned at it, twisting the pages to better capture the light. The journal could truthfully be penned in Lord Justin's hand, and if that were so he was a very good poet and deeply in love with the subject of his verse.

A shiver of distress raced over her skin at

the thought her future husband loved another. But then reason returned. Of course the man was capable of love. He had treated her very gently considering the terrible circumstances they found themselves in. Why shouldn't he have found a woman to love? But still, the thought of marriage to him dimmed somewhat. For the first time she had an inkling of what he must feel about her love for Lord Ramsbury.

Clarry set her fingers to her lips. She hadn't really thought much of Lord Ramsbury these last few days, and in fact, she had only thought of him when Justin had brought him up in conversation. Mostly, she'd been thinking of her future husband and the sensations she experienced when in his arms. Clarry rubbed her arms briskly.

Well, sitting around dwelling on what she couldn't have wouldn't help her at all. She needed to do something. Idleness had never appealed. Clarry tucked the journal into its usual hiding place, scooped up the scrap of parchment, and hurried to the connecting door. She managed to return the scrap of parchment to Justin's desk without incident then headed towards the gardens. There was a lovely walk to the side of the house she longed to explore. Living here at Staplehurst Hall had some advantages. At least she could stride about for the exercise without fear of censure.

As she hurried along a well used path leading away from the Hall, footsteps sounded behind her. She turned to find her future husband hurrying to catch up. Clarry stopped. "My lord, is something amiss?"

"Where are you going?"

Clarry gestured to the woodland path ahead. "I am attempting to take a walk. Is that not allowed?"

Lord Justin scowled. "It isn't if you're headed for the dower house in that great a hurry."

Clarry set her hands to her hips. "I like to take a brisk walk each day, but I've been caged in the Hall without leave. Please let me continue on my way."

Although it appeared Lord Justin wasn't inclined to believe her at first he nodded. "I will come with you. I could do with the exercise myself."

Justin fell into step beside her and because she kept her pace brisk enough to match his longer strides they had soon covered almost a mile in silence. As they crested a rise, Clarry stopped to catch her breath. Lord Justin snaked his arm about her waist. "Do you really enjoy walking that fast or were you hoping to outrun me."

Annoyed not to be believed, Clarry scowled at her future husband. His reaction, to laugh at her expression, surprised her. She could almost believe him happy. He pulled her close against his chest and swung her off her feet and in a tight circle. "My girl, you could wither a man's privates with that expression."

As her feet settled to the ground Clarry took in his amusement but a chill settled over her. "We will have a very bad sort of life if you do not trust me." She fiddled with his cravat. "I had no intention of meeting with your brother. I will be bound to you under the worst circumstances but I promise not to be more of an embarrassment."

Justin dragged her closer, peering intently into her face. A blush heated her cheeks at his close scrutiny. She closed her eyes. Justin pressed his lips to her brow. "I'm not embarrassed. If anything, I think I might be reconciled to the idea."

"Reconciled?"

Lord Justin sighed above her head then settled his chin to the top of her hair. "Content then."

Clarry fought to hold back a relieved grin and pressed her hands flat to his wide chest. A bubble of happiness had claimed her and she silently vowed to increase his contentment somehow. "Could we keep walking do you think?"

"Surely. Where would you like to go?"

Clarry turned around and looked into the next little valley. "Down there. I think I see a stream amongst the trees."

"I know just the path to take." He held out his hand and she laid hers across his palm. "There is a deep hole down there my brother and I used to swim in as boys. I still like to go there when I need some peace."

Although, Clarry noted the hard edge to Justin's mention of his brother, she ignored it. To learn anything about the man she would wed would undoubtedly bring up his brother in conversation. She'd just have to learn to ignore Lord Ramsbury. She smiled encouragingly and tugged him down the hill.

They walked along, side by side when they could, Justin leading her by the hand when they couldn't. For a time she forgot her troubles and concentrated on the warm fingers curled protectively around hers. Lord Justin continued to confuse her. One minute so soft and gentle, the next bristling, as if he'd remembered her entrapment and meant to despise her. She really shouldn't be surprised but she couldn't equate the angry man with her lover. He made her forget everything when he touched her.

Clarry's head jerked up when they stopped. "Oh, it's so lovely here." But she shivered as a chill wind rushed over her exposed skin. "Somewhat colder than the ridge top."

"Too cold for a swim. But when summer is full upon us it's delightfully private here." Lord Justin struggled from his jacket. "Do you swim by the way?"

Clarry stared at the dark, slow moving water. "No, never. Father wouldn't allow me to cavort in public like that. He only barely allowed me to accompany the duchess boating last spring. I've never gotten more than my fingertip wet in a stream."

Lord Justin's heavy jacket settled over her shoulders. She glanced up to find his face inches from hers. A teasing smile lifted his lips. "Then you shall have to learn. I should like to swim with you."

"I'd rather not be dragged under and drowned by my fashions, thank you very much."

Justin's hand curled around her head. "Ah, but you see that is the beauty of allowing me to teach you. I wouldn't let you wear a stitch of clothing so there would be less risk of accidental drowning. I wouldn't let anything bad happen to you."

Clarry's breath rushed from her lungs as he dipped his head and covered her mouth with his. As his tongue invaded, she imagined the scandalous activity. Swimming naked next to her husband, his hands clutching her bare skin tight against his to keep her afloat. Clarry's hands tightened on his lapels.

Justin's lips parted from hers. "Never fear. I'd be naked too. Couldn't bear to have you becoming lonely. Besides, I've heard it's possible to make love suspended in water. I'm dying to discover if it's true."

Clarry pushed at his chest. "You cannot be serious. In there?"

Justin settled her tight against his chest. "I've given the matter serious consideration and have decided that we must make love whenever we can. There should be at least as much pleasure as we can stand from the union for us both."

Clarry stifled a laugh. How serious he sounded. Making love to him had hardly been a chore so far. If anything, she craved more of his touch right now. Clarry let her fingers wander downward until they found the edge of his waistcoat. Justin's breath hitched as she curled her arms around his waist, following the deliciously soft silk.

"Perhaps we should sit." Justin remarked

but Clarry had another idea. She splayed her fingers wide and dropped her hands so they covered his bottom. When she squeezed, Justin claimed her lips again. His rough kiss and hard hands thrilled her. Gone was the polite gentleman of the morning. She'd found the rogue she would marry.

She liked the rogue better.

Justin groaned as she kneaded his rear, then with a frantic rush he hiked up her skirts and grabbed her leg. His fingers burned her bare skin so badly that Clarry wanted more. She slipped her fingers into the back of his trousers. The long tail of his linen shirt impeded her progress to touch his skin and she whimpered impatiently.

"Damn it. Someone is coming."

As Clarry returned to the world, she caught sight of Lord Ramsbury and the man she thought might be Lord Roderick. Mortified by how they might appear to others, she buried her head in his cravat and prayed they didn't join them.

"Ho, Justin," one called, "Don't let us stop you enjoying the lass." That didn't sound like Lord Ramsbury at all. Justin uttered a curse harsh enough to curl Clarry's hair. She peeked around him in time to see Justin's brother fling an arm across the other man's chest and halt their approach. The viscount appeared uneasy so Clarry moved away from Justin to offer him an encouraging smile. After all, they would be family soon.

The viscount didn't smile back. He glanced at Justin then turned his back, giving Clarry the cut direct. Tears filled her eyes as he stalked off in a rush and soon disappeared from sight. She glanced up at Justin to gauge his reaction to his brother's fast leave taking, but he had stiffened and wouldn't look at her either.

After a more than a few painful moments, Clarry tugged his sleeve. "Justin?"

The growl he uttered made her jump. "Perhaps you should return to the house. I have a matter to discuss with my friend, Miss Wheaton, before you are formally introduced to Lord Roderick. After today, an introduction may not be necessary at all."

Miss Wheaton? Clarry turned fully to face her future husband but he avoided meeting her gaze and hurried to his friend. Stung by the sudden dismissal, Clarry watched him conversing with Lord Roderick. Was she not good enough to meet his friend? Occasionally, Lord Justin's head turned until their gazes almost connected but he turned back to the conversation without acknowledging her continued presence. The snub from Justin hurt more than the direct cut from his brother.

Heart pounding in confusion, Clarry had no choice but to turn away to trudge up the long hill alone. She didn't understand what she'd done to make Justin angrier than he may have already been. She'd only tried to be polite. A hard thing given the circumstances they'd been found in. Her with her skirts above her knees and behaving like a common whore.

CHAPTER NINE

"I SAY, Justin, is everything all right there?" Roddy stepped into Justin's line of vision, blocking Clarry's rapid retreat from his sight.

Justin leaned sideways and watched until she disappeared over the rise. Once she had gone he let out the breath he'd held. "Yes, of course. I'll introduce you later." Much, much later. Despite Clarry's near swooning at the sight of his brother, Justin would do his best to protect her from Roddy.

His friend's eyes narrowed. "About the marriage. Do you love the girl?"

Justin snorted. "Of course not. I'm not such a fool to wed a woman for her heart. She has a splendid dowry." The lie burned and coiled around his mouth so strongly that he almost spat. He hoped Roddy believed him so they could talk about other matters.

Roddy smacked his hands together and rubbed them briskly. "So. You'll have funds to spare at last. Well done. Well done. We'll have to find a good use for them. Perhaps replace that nag you ride."

In all honestly, Pericles suited Justin perfectly. The gelding had an unexcitable temperament that suited his habit of composing on horseback. Any other horse would have walked him into a tree due to his inattention. "Perhaps. What say you to a trip into town? I have a mind to spend an evening away from the Hall."

Roddy slapped him on the back. "Excellent. You know, I had feared that marriage might turn you into a stodgy lapdog. Let's head for town, find a table in the tavern and some willing lasses to spend the evening with. If we're lucky we can deprive some poor sap of his blunt just as always, eh?"

Justin forced a smile to his lips. "Let's go."

The quicker he could get away the better he would feel. Clarry had clearly not forgotten her love for his brother and until that happened, Justin would keep his distance. He doubted his heart could stand the strain much longer. He refused to become one of those bitter men he often heard about, fighting duels over a worthless woman's honor until he was made a laughing stock to all.

As the Hall drew near, he spotted his mother at her window, hands on her hips. God only knew what that was about, but he wasn't going to hang about to get involved.

He changed direction and headed directly for the stable to make their escape.

Two hours later, all felt right with the world again. They had secured a corner table in the tavern where Lord Roddy held court. So far they'd attracted a sizeable crowd of the local gentry and more than enough willing ladies to pass about. The blonde on his knee jiggled her breasts close to his face.

"Can I tempt ya, Lord Justin?"

Although Sally had performed admirably the last time he'd had her beneath him, Justin picked up his tankard and pretended he didn't hear. For one thing, it was still early in the evening. For another, even with her perfectly shaped breast close to his mouth he wasn't tempted in the slightest. He wanted Clarry's full heavy breasts in his hands, her curves cradling him close. Sally's scrawny backside dug into his thigh and he adjusted her to ease the discomfort, then adjusted her some more until she found other set of willing hands to curl about her.

Roddy peered over Sally's head and frowned. Justin shook his head, forcing a smile to his lips at relinquishing the girl to Roddy's enjoyment. He didn't want her or anyone else. He wanted Clarry. He made his way out the back door, pretending to be heading for the privy but turned away for the walled enclosure. The kitchen garden was so quiet that he let out a breath, relieved to be alone with his thoughts.

He was doomed for a miserable life.

The conviction that Clarry still loved his brother cut deep into his soul. Perhaps he should move away from the district as his father suggested. At least they might stand a small hope of being content.

Footsteps crunched on gravel and a dark shape joined him. "Jus..."

"Tris..." When a flask appeared before him, Justin accepted it and downed the contents whole.

"I apologize for interrupting you and Miss Wheaton earlier."

Justin passed the empty flask back and leaned against the wall. "There's no need."

"But I interrupted at an inopportune time."

Justin shook his head, and the stars left trails of light behind them in his vision. "Despite what you think you saw, nothing has changed. The woman loves you."

"Are you sure about that now? It seems to

me you were making spectacular progress with her."

Justin stood and took a few steps. The world held steady and he could still feel his broken heart. *Not drunk enough yet.* He turned to glance at his brother's face. The face his future wife adored. "Lust and love are not the same, Tristan. As a newly married man, you should still remember the difference."

Justin stepped back into the tavern and picked up another tankard. Tonight, his only company would be himself and an ale barrel. But he was aware that Tristan hovered anxiously across the room, watching him drown his sorrows in the bitter tasting brew.

Clarry lifted her head from the pillow at the sound of rapid footsteps approaching her door. She held her breath hoping that Justin had come home so she could find out what exactly she'd done to offend him earlier. Despite all her ponderings, she was no closer to understanding him. When she'd received a note from the duchess saying that she was otherwise engaged for the evening and that Clarry could eat alone in her room she had jumped at the chance. A few hours of privacy were a blessing.

But when she'd discovered that Justin had left her alone at the Hall she'd begun to fret. She hadn't seen him or anyone in hours, except for servants bringing her dinner. The silence made her uncomfortable.

A soft knock made her jump, but the door swung open before she had a chance to call out in return. The duchess hurried forward. "Well?"

Clarry glanced around her. Well what? Had she forgotten something important she was meant to do for the duchess? She could remember every awkward conversation they'd shared up till now and at no time had the duchess asked her for anything. However, her mind was too full with worry over Justin right now to care if she'd disappointed the dragon. "Well what, Your Grace?"

The duchess hopped up onto the bed beside her. Clarry gaped as Justin's mother swung her feet two and fro. The movement hypnotized. "I understand that you and Justin quarreled today?"

Had they? She knew she'd been dismissed out of hand as an unwanted companion. But quarrel? Didn't it take two to make an argument? "I couldn't say, Your Grace?"

The duchess continued to swing her feet.

"We will have to do something about that, too, eventually. But right now we have a bigger decision to make. What are you going to do?"

Clarry wrenched her gaze away from the duchess's pink satin slippers and shook her head. "I don't know what you are talking about, Your Grace." She slipped from the bed and threw her shawl about her shoulders.

The duchess heaved a heavy sigh. "What are you going to do about loving my son?"

Clarry's breath caught. "Justin told you?"

"Of course not. Most men would not admit out loud that love existed let alone mention the topic to his mother. But Justin is different. He has waited for love to tap his shoulder all his life. However, I do think you should tell him just so there is no misunderstanding. He deserves the truth before your vows are spoken."

Clarry plunked down on a chair as the air left her lungs. "Justin knows already. And he's prepared to overlook it and marry me anyway."

The duchess snorted. "Overlook that the woman he loves more than his last breath loves him back. Does madness run in your family, my dear?"

Clarry shook her head again. The duchess was going to be vastly unhappy but Clarry couldn't let her misunderstand the situation any longer. "Lord Justin is well aware of my affection for Lord Ramsbury. He's known that from the start of this whole horrid business."

The duchess's feet stopped swinging. "You love both my sons? How extraordinary."

"No, no, no, Your Grace. I only love one."

"And which one would that be. The one who is forever beyond reach or the one you're waiting up for like a homeless hound. Justin has bent over backward to make you happy and comfortable here. And yet, the night before the wedding, it is he who has run away to drown his sorrows and not you."

Clarry's chest burned. "The night before—"

"The duke has returned earlier than expected with the special license. No matter. The nuptials between you and Justin will be held at eleven tomorrow, regardless of the state of my sons head. After all the moaning and whimpering the pair of you have uttered in this room there is no chance of delay or escape. So don't even consider changing your mind, Clarry."

At the duchess's use of her shortened given name, Clarry looked up, studying the duchess. Despite the threat that had just crossed her lips, Her Grace appeared giddy with happiness. She fairly jumped from the bed and crossed the room to cup her hands about Clarry's face. She smiled a little dreamily then drew Clarry into her arms.

At first, the gentle hug shocked her. But then, after a while, being in the duchess's embrace reminded her of her own long-gone mother and how much she missed such impulsive affection. Clarry rested her hands on the duchess's back and the little woman rocked her as if she were a baby. "My son has the most generous heart, Clarry. Whatever misunderstanding exists between you will be forgiven once you tell him you've discovered where your affections truly lie. Regardless of your misguided infatuation for my eldest son, Justin has loved only you. I may not have recognized you in his poetry from the start but I know see you now. He writes about you constantly. Not ever by name, but you are his muse—his reason for coming home despite the likelihood of rejection."

The duchess's words brought a lump to Clarry throat. She must be mistaken?

Justin had never given a hint his feeling were deeper than that of any other gentleman until she'd thrown herself into the wrong bed. Had he loved her all along and she'd been blinded by Lord Ramsbury's brilliance? Poor Justin. She'd hurt him and she'd never understood what she was doing to him.

She'd clung to the hope for love with a man who never wanted her. Clarry dropped her head to the duchess's shoulder as tears pricked her eyes. Had she really thought love could only be found with a titled husband? Given that she'd failed to even notice Justin's affections before, it was obvious that she had. She was so ashamed of how she'd treated him. The love she'd hoped for her entire life, the one she read about in the pages of Justin's journal, lay within reach after all if only she could fix her mistake.

The duchess patted her back and then set Clarry away from her, her gaze solemn and somewhat watery too. She sniffed. "Now, about the other, more important, matter. I think, given the circumstances of this marriage, that you had better refer to me as Mother from now on. An appearance of familiarity between us will end any gossip when we return to London for the season."

Call the duchess Mother? Maybe she was mad or perhaps she'd fallen asleep and merely dreamed this whole encounter. Clarry shook her head to see if she could awaken. This must all be a frightening illusion.

The duchess frowned. "Has my reputation as a dragon grown so fearsome that you cannot look beyond it? Justin has chosen to remain here at Staplehurst Hall for your benefit. I had hoped not to hear another person Your Grace me at all hours of the day and night. I had once wished for daughters too, a large family, but was blessed with only my sons."

When the duchess put it like that Clarry felt particularly churlish to deny her. She wouldn't be betraying her own mother, wherever she may be, by any familiarity with her future mother-in-law. In fact, Clarry could become used to it. Perhaps she could try it on for size. "I did not mean to give offense, Mother."

The duchess's nose wrinkled. "Hmm, perhaps Mama would be better. Mother sounds extremely dragon like, but we shall see how we get along and adapt if necessary. Now, since everything of importance has been settled, into bed with you young lady. I want you well rested for tomorrow's festivities."

The duchess, Mama, Clarry reminded herself, pushed and bullied until Clarry was tucked tightly into bed. As she stared up at the canopy, the duchess came close with the candle and pressed a light kiss to her brow.

Startled by the motherly peck, Clarry sat up again. "Where's Justin?"

The duchess brushed Clarry's hair back

over her shoulder and let out a disapproving huff. "Deep in his cups at the tavern. Tristan sent word that he is keeping watch over his brother and will see he presents himself for the ceremony tomorrow."

"Why is he drinking tonight? I don't understand why he changed so suddenly today. Everything seemed fine until Lord Roderick arrived."

The duchess touched her cheek gently. "From what I understand, Lord Roderick arrived at the swimming hole with my eldest son. And since Justin still thinks you favor his brother, I am sure your agile mind can understand his anxiety. Men are such fragile creatures and so easy to offend if their desirability is called into question. I suggest you explain your change of heart as soon as you can. Before the wedding, if at all possible. I'd much rather a joyous ceremony than a solemn one. Think about it before morning comes."

Clarry covered her face to hide her embarrassment. "Do you know everything?"

The duchess touched her head. "Not everything at first, but eventually, yes. One of the advantages of my position."

She let herself out and Clarry lay back on her pillows. Justin had loved her all along and she'd been breaking his heart without knowing it. Of course she cared for him now. He'd been so kind. But love? Clarry curled into a ball on her side to consider the matter. Despite the circumstances, he'd had done his best to protect her—even from his mother's earlier fussing. And he did make her feel heavenly. His kisses, his hands, his skills in this very bed had turned her ideas of making love on its head.

Would he still lie with her and cuddle her close as he had done so often these last days when they were older? She did love that. Would any man want to hold her in his arms all night if he doubted he was loved in return?

The thought of lying in this bed with another repulsed her. In fact, now that she considered the matter, she'd be horrified to let Lord Ramsbury see her as Justin had—naked and breathless after his lovemaking. But if the one you love made you that way shouldn't that be acceptable? Did that mean she didn't love Lord Ramsbury, not even a little, anymore? Had she loved him at all, or just loved the idea of being married?

Clarry rolled onto her back and thumped the mattress with both fists. If Justin were here she could talk to him and perhaps they could both sort out this mess. But tonight he was drinking to soothe his bruised pride, and the heart she'd apparently wounded. An effort that might not be necessary at all if she did in fact love him as the duchess claimed. But was it possible to fall completely in love in just three days?

CHAPTER TEN

THE HEAVY IVORY silk gown slid up Clarry's arms and settled into place as if made for her. While the duchess's maid circled behind her back to tie the laces firmly, Clarry stared into the mirror and tried to control her nervousness. She would marry today, at eleven in the duchess's drawing room before the lingering guests from Lord Ramsbury's recent ceremony. There had been half a dozen or so ensconced about the Hall yet other than brief introductions at dinner, Justin and the duchess had kept Clarry well away from them.

Well, she would marry today if Justin did, in fact, return to the hall. His bedchamber had been painfully quiet this morning.

"Drop you hand, Clarry. Enough of that."

Guiltily, Clarry forced her nails down and away from her mouth. She was so nervous that

Justin wouldn't arrive for the ceremony that she'd resumed a childish habit she'd thought long forgotten. The duchess, Mama, had scolded her twice already since she'd risen from bed. To distract herself, Clarry fingered the seed pearls adorning her décolleté. The stunning gown had transformed her from merely pretty to a princess in wait for her prince. She'd hardly recognized herself. "I cannot thank you enough for the gown, Mama. I never imagined I'd wear something so fine."

The duchess fussed with the sleeves. "A bride deserves something pretty on her wedding day. Your mother would have taken care of the matter beautifully. Jane has excellent taste."

Clarry frowned at the mention of her mother's name. She'd stopped thinking about her a long time ago except occasionally. Her abandonment still hurt, even if she'd come to realize that staying with her father would have crushed her spirit completely.

"Now, I have a few matters to take care of before the ceremony—"

"Such as ensure Justin comes," Clarry whispered.

The duchess slipped an arm around her shoulders and squeezed. "Tristan says that he's awake and reeling from a dreadful head, but will be delivered on time as promised. I probably shouldn't pass this along but Tristan had to dump a bucket of cold water over Justin's head to wake him. It's been an eventful morning at the dower house."

Poor Justin. Of all the indignities to suffer through on his wedding day. She'd have to make it up to him tonight. She would have him go to sleep a happier man than he'd awoken. The anticipation curled her lips into a wide smile. Beside her, the duchess chuckled then hurried away.

Tonight she would be Justin's wife until death parted them. Clarry curled her hand over her belly as excitement filled her. She would be Justin's. She would wake beside him sometimes, make love to him as often as she could tempt him, and hope he'd come to trust her enough to read his beautiful poetry to her before he showed anyone else. But she had to tell him she knew about that. She had to return the journal.

"Hello beautiful," a male voice drawled.

Clarry spun about, startled out of her daydreaming.

Lord Roderick lounged against the doorway, leering at her. "I don't believe we've been introduced. Lord Roderick at your service, Miss Wheaton. I'm a very good friend of your future husband."

"I've heard of you, Lord Roderick."

He pushed off the wall. "Please, call me, Roddy. All my close acquaintances do." Lord Roderick paced closer and peered about the room. "And we are going to become quite close, my dear. As close as two people can be in fact."

He'd come to collect on the wager. Although Clarry's stomach tumbled over, she had to hide that he intimidated her. She knew what he wanted. The journal or, if he didn't get that, he planned to lie with her. She couldn't give him Justin's journal and she certainly wouldn't lie with him. He disgusted her.

Rather than play cat and mouse, Clarry decided to attack the situation head on. He thought himself irresistible. She'd prove otherwise. "I take it you've come to claim your winnings, Lord Roderick."

The man stopped moving. His gaze raked her from head to foot, setting her resolve on its edge. She could do this. She could dissuade him from claiming the bet.

A slow smile lit his face. "You know of the bet already don't you, my dear?"

"Yes." Clarry clenched her hands together, very aware the gesture conveyed her distress. But she had to do something with them other than hitch up her skirts and bolt from the chamber. She wouldn't become a plaything to Justin's questionable acquaintance.

Lord Roderick smiled wolfishly. "Well now. That will make life much simpler. Hand over the journal or pay the piper his due."

Clarry licked her lips. "The journal is lost, I'm told. I certainly don't have it." Actually the journal was six feet away from where she stood, tucked into its usual spot under a pillow. It called to her. She fixed her gaze on the man before her instead.

Lord Roderick sucked in a deep breath. "Well then, I imagine you've reconciled yourself to the alternative. Let's have at it then."

He took a step forward but stopped when Clarry flung up her hand. At least he could be stopped. She couldn't deal with an animal. "What guarantees are you prepared to offer me in return?"

"Guarantees?" He flung his head back and laughed. "I've never had a woman doubt my prowess before. Don't worry, little mouse, you'll wish to be marrying me by the end and not Justin."

Clarry could not believe that would be true. She didn't find this man remotely pleasing. Not the way Justin was. "I imagine our opinions might differ on that subject since I appear to have no say in this debauching. But do you simply expect me to lie still while you rob me of my very life?"

"Woman, I'm not planning on killing you. Merely taking my fun in your arms for a romp. In fact, I can quite see why Justin was so out of sorts last night. Must be quite a strain, resisting taking you to his bed."

Relief coursed through Clarry. Justin hadn't told his friend exactly why they were to marry so swiftly. Lord Roderick appeared to have no idea Justin had bedded her either. But how could that work to her advantage if he thought her pure?

A sudden thought popped into her head. "What if you're diseased?"

Lord Roderick drew back as if she'd slapped him. "I've not got the bloody pox, woman. I'm not that bad a friend."

Not much of a friend at all to want to seduce a man's future wife. But she had to keep him off balance. "Really? Yet you intend to force me into that bed."

When she waved her arm in that direction, his eyes lit with anticipation. Curses. She'd lost ground again.

"You're not his wife yet. And he agreed to the bet. My honor demands satisfaction."

Clarry circled him, hoping her movements appeared the result of nervousness not imminent flight. "Well, my honor demands proof that you are as healthy as a horse."

He took another step back. "I beg your pardon."

Honestly, anyone watching them must think them inventing some new dance. But the threat to her virtue was very real. She would not let this man touch her. The bedchamber door lay evenly between them now. She'd have to move quickly and surprise him to outdistance his longer legs if she tried to escape. "You heard me. I want proof that you are as free of illness. It is my intention to give Justin a son and I cannot do that if you disease me."

Lord Roderick scratched at his jaw. "The only way to do that, my dear, is to be on intimate terms." His smile widened again. "On the bed with you then."

"I may be young and innocent, but I'm not so foolish as to fall for that." And not such a fool as to move away from the door. "Proof can be provided right here." She cocked her head to the side. "I'm waiting."

Eventually, Lord Roderick caught her meaning and a wicked smile crossed his face. She steeled herself as his hand reached for the buttons of his trousers. As his shirt lifted and disappeared under his waistcoat, Clarry held her breath. She let it go with a whoosh when Lord Roderick dropped his trousers suddenly, exposing himself to the light.

He stood still and let her look her fill.

She gaped. "That's it?" Goodness! Justin was much better proportioned when aroused.

His hands dropped from his hips. "I beg your pardon?"

Clarry took a step closer. "Really? Is that all you're going to put in me. Honestly, I thought you must have had a formidable staff to have made such a bet. How terribly mundane." Her eyes strayed and caught on a tattoo etched into his upper right thigh. Despite her curiosity, Clarry chuckled to grind insult deeper.

Lord Roderick's face heated. "How dare you?" Although the hissed words sounded as gruff as her father when he had his dander up, his stance hinted at discomfort. He covered his groin with his hands.

Now she might just be winning. Clarry shook her head. "That's like a pot calling the kettle black, isn't it?" When Lord Roddy made no move to continue Clarry cleared her throat. "The terms of the bet have been met, Lord Roderick. This is as intimate as we will ever be. I am aware of your proportions, small as they are. I believe you may leave me now."

When he didn't move, she glanced down at his thigh. "Is that a tattoo of a woman's name?"

Lord Roderick quickly tugged his trousers

up over his hips. "Who are you to gaze upon a naked man and not even flinch?"

"I am Lord Justin's already, my lord." She smiled at how good that felt to say aloud. "Anything else offered is simply not enough to tempt me. We will not speak of this matter again, but I will not hesitate to spread the intelligence that you have a woman's name tattooed on your skin if word of our meeting ever spreads. Beth. Would that be the missing Lady Elizabeth by any chance?" I do hope we understand each other, my lord?"

Lord Roderick scowled as he finished dressing. "That we do."

When the door slammed behind his back, Clarry sagged into a chair. Goodness that had been dreadful. Necessary, but dreadful. She would not have that scoundrel laughing at her for years to come whenever they met. She hoped he'd avoid her like the plague. Clarry took another deep breath.

"That was very well played," the duchess said as she clapped her hands.

Oh no, the duchess. Clarry turned to face her future mother-in-law. "You heard?"

"Heard and saw it all. What there was, of course. Risky, but well played. I cannot imagine Lord Roderick ever approaching you with anything but the utmost respect from now on."

Clarry gulped. "I couldn't give him Justin's journal."

The duchess grinned. "Because you love my son."

"I couldn't lie with him either."

"Because you love my son and couldn't bear another to touch you as he does."

The duchess's repetitions could get on her nerves quite easily. Clarry frowned. Did she really love Justin after only four days? With the proof of her own actions before her, Clarry conceded that she did feel more for him than she originally imagined possible.

The duchess patted her clenched fingers. "You do not need to admit to such feelings to me, but you should admit them to yourself and to Justin that you do not love his brother. Not every woman knows there own heart in the beginning—or at the end for that matter. Marriage is a painful experience when you are plagued with doubts."

Puzzled by the duchess's last comment, Clarry asked a question that had troubled her for some time. "Do you not love the duke?"

The duchess rocked back on her heels, lips pressed tight together.

"Forgive me. That was an inexcusable question to ask you."

The duchess closed her eyes. "Our marriage

was arranged by our families. I had a large dowry and the dukedom had large debts."

Clarry closed the gap between them and caught the duchess's cold fingers in hers. "I'm sorry. That must have been an uncomfortable beginning."

"Oh, being a duchess has its perks. I get to have my way somewhat more often than most wives." A smile tugged her lips. "Now, enough of my problems, I have a surprise visitor for you."

The duchess rushed off while Clarry tried to stem the ache from the words the duchess hadn't uttered. What a horror it would be to never love or feel comfortable with the man you married. To never feel peace with the life you had to live.

When the door opened again, Clarry turned, expecting to see her future mother-in-law. She gaped and then fell back in the chair again.

CHAPTER ELEVEN

JUSTIN STRODE up the steps of Staplehurst Hall flanked by his brother and his pregnant sister-in-law. He needed their support today. Despite the pain Clarry might feel over Tristan's presence, he wanted his brother to stand up with him.

Brinkley let him in, a relieved smile pasted on the old butler's face. "Welcome home, Lord Justin. The other gentlemen are waiting in the library until the ladies are ready."

"Thank you.' He turned for the library, conscious of Tristan kissing his wife farewell behind his back. Pain tightened his chest. A morning spent with the newlyweds had proved uncomfortable. Their obvious affection—a knife twisting in his heart.

"Justin, my boy, you look dreadful."

"Thank you, Father."

Justin took the brandy offered but nursed the glass rather than drank it. His head pounded bad enough as it was. He glanced around and found Roddy standing somewhat away from everyone else. He crossed the room to join him. "I lost track of you last night."

Roddy's hand shook as he lowered his glass. "Not surprising. You hit the amber pretty hard last night. I'm surprised you can stand."

Justin gestured toward his brother. "Tristan is hard to ignore when he pours ice cold water over your head."

"Remind me never to spend time with your brother." His eyes narrowed. "Were you reluctant to marry today?'

"No. No of course not. I just drank to much last night. Clarry's dowry is worth any shackle about my leg."

Roddy peered at him oddly. "She is something, isn't she?"

Justin's head cleared. "You were introduced?"

Roddy winced. "Let us just say I had the opportunity to introduce myself earlier today. A decision I'm regretting. She is not quite what I expected for you but congratulations. You will have an interesting marriage."

"Thank you." What the hell had happened while he'd been gone? He glanced toward the door wondering if he could seek Clarry out before the ceremony to be sure she was still here and not upset. Who knew what Roddy would have said if they were truly alone.

"Oh, and the wager is paid in full."

Justin's vision turned red as he snapped his attention back to Roddy. "You have my journal?"

"No. She said it was lost. Did she lie to me and put me through hell for her own amusement?"

Justin's fingers curled into a fist. "What happened this morning?"

"Steady there, old boy. You'll burst your head with all that hot headedness." Roddy looked left and right as he backed himself into a corner. "Luscious as she is, nothing happened. But you'd do well to stay on her good side."

Justin uncurled his fingers suddenly, aware that Tristan had hold of his arm. "If you touched one hair on her head I'll disembowel you where you stand."

"Justin," Tristan warned. "Lower your voice. There are other people in the room. Your future father in law for one."

Justin forced himself to relax. Roddy had

promised that nothing had happened and he was many things but not a liar. "Perhaps you should recall a sudden appointment, Roddy. I don't think I'd care for your presence at my wedding after all."

Roddy nodded, but his mouth twisted with bitterness. "As you wish." He bowed then hurried for the door. When he had disappeared from sight, Justin glanced at his brother.

Tristan raised one brow. "What was that about, Jus? I hope to god I misheard."

"I need to see Clarry. Can you find mother and arrange it?" Justin scraped his hand through his hair, and tried not to groan aloud.

His brother nodded and headed off. When he returned to the outside hall and cocked his head, Justin slipped from the room unnoticed and headed to the room Tristan indicated. The door shut with a soft thud behind his back.

Her dark head popped around the back of a chair. "There you are. I was beginning to worry."

"Clarry." He hurried forward and fell to his knees, taking in the stunning gown she'd be wearing for the wedding with a bare glance. "What happened with Roddy?"

Her button nose crinkled up in distaste. "I repaid the debt, but not in the way he wanted.

As I understood the terms of your bet, I had to either hand over your journal or be intimate with him." Her hand rose, holding out his journal. "I couldn't let him embarrass you. This is too private for public consumption."

Justin took the journal from her but his heart pounded. "They were just words, Clarry. You are more important than a book."

"Not when those beautiful words are about a man's love for a woman. You are a wonderful poet, Justin. I have treasured that book since it came into my keeping."

When she raised his hand to her lips and kissed his knuckles, Justin quaked. "I wrote about you. I've loved you so long. But I never told you because you loved Tristan instead."

"Who?" Her face twisted in confusion. "I've only loved one man in my entire life, Justin Greene, and he's kneeling at my feet this very minute."

Justin scowled. "You didn't love me before."

"Hmm, you are right about that. I've been mulling over my behavior all night and this morning and I've come to the conclusion that I don't love Lord Ramsbury at all. I would never want to kiss him. Or share his bed. And I spent the whole night worrying about you. Where you were? What you were doing? Why you were not in my bed making love to me? All those questions kept me awake last night. I missed you dreadfully and I was so afraid you wouldn't come to marry me this morning."

Justin gulped over the hard lump forming in his throat. Clarry's confession was more than he'd ever hoped to hear. "You missed me?"

Clarry smiled, leaned forward and kissed him. He dropped the journal to the floor and curled his fingers about her skull, careful not to disturb her beautifully arranged hair. When she drew back her expression was dreamy. "You ruined me for anyone else."

As much as he tried, he couldn't stop his eyes from misting over at her confession. He closed them and kissed Clarry again, drinking in her desire and the beginning's of a love he'd only dreamed about.

Clarry threaded her fingers through his hair and held him close. "Are their any more wagers waiting for me on the other side of the wedding ceremony, Justin?"

"No. I promise there's not." He sat back on his heels. "I need to know what happened this morning between you and Roddy."

Her face scrunched up again. "It wasn't pleasant. He surprised me in my bedchamber."

Justin curled his hands into fists, quite prepared to leave Clarry and pound the scoundrel into pulp. Clarry cupped his face between his hands. "I demanded something of my own in the bargain, Justin. I demanded to know he was free of disease. The idea of it seemed to offend him but he dropped his pants and I—I laughed."

Justin leaned back. "You laughed at Roddy's privates."

"I couldn't help it. I was so anxious but he had this tattoo of a woman's name beside it and I lost my head. He seemed offended by my laughter and he left."

"I should be furious with you for that."

"Mama said it had been a risky move but it worked nonetheless and he never touched me."

"Mama?"

Clarry smiled impishly. "The duchess has insisted I call her by a less formal name. We've settled on mama instead of mother."

Mother and Clarry had buried the hatchet while his back was turned. Dear God.

Clarry laughed suddenly at his expression. "Isn't it better this way, Justin?"

"Yes, its better, but—"

"Have I made too big a mess of everything for you to be comfortable again? I had thought you would be pleased that the distressing matters were dealt with swiftly."

When Clarry bit her lower lip, stopping the

wobble that had begun, he leaned in to kiss her uncertainty away. He loved this impulsive woman so much that he'd probably go mad without her. It didn't matter that she'd managed to solve his problem and stun him within a few short minutes. He'd come to grow used to the sensation eventually.

A knock sounded on the door. "Justin," his mother called. "It's eleven. The vicar and our guests are assembled in the drawing room."

He ran his hands along Clarry's legs, hearing the hitch to her breathing as his thumbs traced a path along the inside of her thighs. The look she gave him, so full of longing scorched him. "The vicar is waiting, my love."

Her fingers curled over his and squeezed. "We shouldn't keep such an important man waiting."

No they shouldn't. But they both wanted to.

Justin stood, tugged Clarry to her feet and held out his arm. "Shall we?"

When her arm curled about his Justin drew her to the door and along the hall towards the drawing room. Although he'd expected Mr. Wheaton to be waiting for Clarry, the woman standing alone surprised him.

Clarry leaned into his arm. "Mama summoned my mother for the wedding. She's going to watch from here so Father doesn't see her and raise a fuss."

So this was Clarry's long lost mother. The other woman seemed tired, but she smiled at them warmly. Justin smiled, too, but she didn't approach. She lingered beside the wall, casting furtive glances along the hall toward the drawing room. Clarry touched his arm. "We should hurry along now before Father loses his patience and comes looking for us."

At Clarry's urging they approached the drawing room door together and just inside the threshold, Justin relinquished her to Mr. Wheaton. He took two paces away before he turned back. "Clarry, how did you get my journal?"

The impish smile she cast beyond his left shoulder startled him. "Why from the duchess, of course. Her Grace gave it to me months ago and said the poet would appeal to me."

Justin glanced at his mother, and back at Clarry. "Did she now?"

Clarry leaned closer to whisper, "Is she always right?"

Justin pressed his lips to Clarry's again. "I am beyond relieved that she is, Mrs. Greene."

Clarry's eyes sparkled. "I'm not Mrs. Greene yet. But give me a minute or two and you'll never be rid of me."

"Sounds perfect to me." Justin turned and caught the guests craning their necks to hear every word. He didn't care in the least. He had a woman who loved him. She truly did.

The End

WILD RANDALLS SERIES

Engaging the Enemy ~ Forsaking the Prize

Guarding the Spoils ~ Hunting the Hero

*

SAINTS AND SINNERS SERIES

The Duke and I ~ A Gentleman's Vow

An Earl of Her Own ~ The Lady Tamed

*

REBEL HEARTS SERIES

The Wedding Affair ~ An Affair of Honor

The Christmas Affair ~ An Affair so Right

*

MISS MAYHEM SERIES

Miss Watson's First Scandal

Miss George's Second Chance

Miss Radley's Third Dare

Miss Merton's Last Hope

USA Today Bestselling Author Heather Boyd believes every character she creates deserves their own happily-ever-after—no matter how much trouble she puts them through. With that goal in mind, she writes steamy romances that skirt the boundaries of propriety to keep readers enthralled until the wee hours of the morning. Heather has published over fifty regency romance novels and shorter works full of daring seductions and distinguished rogues. She lives north of Sydney, Australia, with her trio of rogues and a four-legged overlord.

Learn more about Heather at:
Heather-Boyd.com